Ancient
Stories for
Modern Times

Ancient Stories for Modern Times

50 SHORT WISDOM TALES FOR ALL AGES

Retold by
Faye Mogensen

Skinner House Books
Boston

www.skinnerhouse.org

Printed in the United States

Cover design by Kathryn Sky-Peck
Text design by Jeff Miller

print ISBN: 978-1-55896-779-3

6 5 4 3 2
21

Library of Congress Cataloging-in-Publication Data

Names: Mogensen, Faye, author.
Title: Ancient stories for modern times : 50 short wisdom tales for all ages
    / Faye Mogensen.
Description: Boston : Skinner House Books, 2016. | Includes bibliographical
    references.
Identifiers: LCCN 2016003640 (print) | LCCN 2016011986 (ebook) |
    ISBN 9781558967793 (pbk. : alk. paper) | ISBN 9781558967809
Subjects: LCSH: Conduct of life—Miscellanea. | Wisdom—Miscellanea.
Classification: LCC BJ1548 .M585 2016 (print) | LCC BJ1548 (ebook) |
    DDC 170/.44—dc23
LC record available at http://lccn.loc.gov/2016003640

Contents

Living with One Another

Practicing Generosity

Seeking Justice

Developing Perspective

Accepting Change

Seeking Peace and Finding Hope

Foreword

A LOVER OF FOLKTALES experiences many pleasures, not the least of which is discovering a new wise tale or hearing a familiar story told from a perspective that sparks new insight. As a professional storyteller and author of two collections of world tales, I've spent many a satisfying day pouring through folktale indexes and collections or listening to other tellers in search of those priceless gems of wisdom. And so it was with satisfied delight that I read *Ancient Stories for Modern Times*. It is replete with such surprises, told with imagination and heart.

Stories are gifts passed down to us from previous generations. As I research stories from many cultures and spiritual traditions, I find the same motifs or themes repeated over and over. These are the themes that have been worth passing down through the evolution of tale-telling. Their messages have survived the test of time because they are the ones we need to hear in order to live peacefully with one another and with the earth. I was heartened to see that the themes, principles, and qualities Faye Mogensen has chosen to promulgate are the ones most needed to heal ourselves, our relationships, and our world.

While searching for tales I have often been guilty of consuming them much like candy, thereby missing the opportunity to let their wisdom work in or through me. In these times of media saturation, we may all fall victim to this kind of loss. How often have I been invited to bring stories to a school only to have the students hurried off at the end without the chance to ponder and share the story's wisdom. When a story is heard and time is not given to internalize it, its gifts can be missed. I so appreciated Mogensen's evocative questions for reflection following each story. They inspire thoughtfulness and exploration. I can hear the listeners sharing personal stories after the telling and envisioning new ways to bring the values we hold dear into action.

Training teachers, storytellers, and parents to tell stories to audiences of all ages has taught me to have great respect for the unique gifts and strengths that each individual brings to the telling of a tale. Mogensen is clearly a seasoned teller and generous teacher. She promotes respect for the stories, their sources, and the new teller's ability to share a tale effectively. Her "Tips for Telling" invite the teller to relax and be present with the story, and give sage advice on how to "love the story, love the audience, and love oneself." The "Story Maps" following each story facilitate learning the sequence of events to build the tale around, without having to "memorize" it. They are a gift to new tellers who often see this as the biggest obstacle.

Growing up steeped in a Unitarian church community has shaped my values and leanings toward generosity, justice, and a passion to make the world a better place. It is with gratitude that I write this foreword to *Ancient Stories for Modern Times*. These fine stories for young and old celebrate and demonstrate beautiful values and provide sustenance for putting them into action in the world today.

Elisa Davy Pearmain, author of *Forgiveness: Telling Our Stories in New Ways*, *Once Upon a Time: Storytelling to Teach Character and Prevent Bullying*, *Doorways to the Soul: 52 Wisdom Tales from Around the World*, and *Moral Tales: A Tapestry of Faith Program for Children Grades 2–3* (with Alice Anacheka-Nasemann)

Introduction

"I could never be a storyteller," declared a friend.

Within the next half hour she blurted, "Guess what happened?" and then riveted me with a tale full of tension, foreshadowing, and pregnant pause. I couldn't help but tease her—I tease everyone who claims not to be a storyteller. According to evolutionary psychologists and literary Darwinists, our brains are hardwired to think in terms of stories. It's only within the last few hundred years that a majority of people are able to read, but no training is required for us to learn to tell a story. Storytelling is so instinctive to us that we barely realize we are doing it or that, as we do it, we are organizing our thoughts and making meaning of our experiences. We are naturally compelled to tell stories because they bring pleasure, share knowledge, and offer advice. Through stories we preserve and transmit our memories, our values, and our cultures. This book is an opportunity for me to share my love of learning through story and to help you harness the power of storytelling to touch people's lives.

A study conducted at Stanford University suggests that a story is twenty-two times more memorable than fact. Imagery and twists of plot keep our minds active and engaged. Even more than the mind, stories engage the heart and the spirit, and the old adage that "one story leads to another" is a good description of the source of a story's power. Images and feelings that a story evokes in us help us to recall our own similar stories, and so we internalize its messages, each in our own unique way. We develop empathy because we recognize our own experiences, dreams, strengths, and foibles in other people's stories. When stories expose us to different ways of being, we become more flexible and creative in our responses to the world around us and can be inspired to change and grow. Because their characters often solve challenges through their creativity and discernment, folktales model important lateral or critical thinking skills. In all these ways and more, stories are excellent teachers.

Storytelling Is a Unique Experience

While I credit my mesmerizing storyteller father for having ingrained the art of the oral tale in me, I was reserved as a young adult. It was not until I was required to make public presentations as a park naturalist that I began storytelling—almost by accident. I quickly overcame my nervousness because people were captivated by the stories and seemed only secondarily aware of me. I continue to feel that when a story is told, it's as if the story perches in the space between the audience and the teller, and that in our shared experience, we are present in the moment. Quite literally, an oral story is a *presentation*, or the gift of presence. The direct relationship between the teller and the audience makes the experience special; storytelling feels personal and intimate even when hundreds of people are listening. The story comes alive especially because there is no paper, text, or image to mediate the story or lock it into one form. The audience constantly gives feedback (usually non-verbal) and the story changes, if only just a little. At the same time, the changing story changes the storyteller. Personal stories are a wonderful gift and an excellent means of reflecting on our lives, but that is not the focus of this book. Instead, I offer a multicultural cross section of folktale, mythology, and legend to ponder and share. All of these stories have been retold thousands of times over—each time a little differently.

About Folktales

"Wait a minute," says my friend. "I'm not about to start telling folktales. I couldn't do that. I only tell stories about things I know. That's my limit." I begin to tease her again. "What about Hansel and Gretel?" She blushes. Like the rest of us, my friend has heard folktales of one kind or another, if not through oral telling then through books and movies. We all know the genre and the cadence of these stories. When we hear "once upon a time" or "long ago and far away," we are cued to listen. There's a kind of comfort in entering into this world of story, and although they may seem far removed from the realities of everyday life, their fictional and sometimes fantastical nature can provide a safe means of exploring difficult questions. The ogre or the good fairy portrayed in a story may not be so different from a friend, a neighbor, even ourselves. But because the stories are from another time and place, we are not affronted by their message; we take only what we want or are able to take from the story. Most importantly, we like the stories! With their colorful characters and imaginative plots, they have universal appeal and are perfect for multi-generational audiences. In my thirty years of storytelling, I've noticed that with an in-person storyteller making eye contact, children do not necessarily have to understand everything, especially if there is a refrain or action they can repeat. On the other hand, even the "youngest" story can be enjoyed by adults if it has a meaningful message to convey. In fact, most folktales were originally told to adults. Folktales and legends are different than personal stories, and yet they are similar in the way they can prompt us to reflect on our lives. They are the stories that have stood the test of time, and the most powerful ones are called "wisdom tales." Many are derivatives of ancient mythologies—the stories of the gods and giants retold in the human realm, sometimes with a little magic thrown into the mix. They touch upon universal themes of human pathos, offering us a tool for considering how to best lead our lives.

The Wisdom Tale

I was reminded of the value of the wisdom tale in a very personal way in 2004, when I attended the National Storytelling Network annual conference. During a conversation with another storyteller, I related a personal struggle involving my in-laws. My listener responded, "You're reminding me of 'Grandfather's Wooden Bowl.'" My heart beat in time to her words as she told me the tale. Though the details were nothing like my experience, the story confirmed for me that the decision I made was the right one. The experience triggered memories of another storytelling conference I'd attended several years earlier, where an Okanagan teller shared some of her people's traditional tales and emphatically stated that these stories, though they may be full of exaggeration or comedy, are not just stories, they are teachings. She went on to tell us that, when she was acting stubbornly or selfishly as a little girl, her grandmother would say, "Now you are being like coyote in such and such a story." The process of hearing stories and reflecting on them taught her values and ethics. And her elders used these stories as a gentle way to nudge her into changing her behavior when it was out of line. Together these experiences struck me deeply. I wanted to lead a "storied" life. I wanted to be able to recognize myself in folktales so that I could also gently remind myself to extend kindness, like Pheasant in "Birds Find Friendship," or to be generous, like the mother-in-law in "Polite Peculiarities." I longed for a body of teaching stories that I could turn to that would guide me in becoming my best self with humor and grace. The problem for those of us who've grown up in Western secular culture, in families of multiple cultural origins, is that we don't have a single resource to draw from. In fact, there are an endless and almost dizzying number of possibilities.

I have found inspiration in some of these wonderful story collections; several of my favorite titles are listed in the sources, and many of the stories that I've learned from and tell are in these books.

Why This Book?

Over the last eighteen years, I've been involved in the Unitarian Universalist movement, first as a congregant and currently as the director of spiritual learning at the First Unitarian Church of Victoria, British Columbia. In worship services for all ages and in the children's program, I tell a particular kind of story that is generally not much more than five minutes long and relates in some way to one or more of the seven Unitarian Universalist Principles. I've come to realize that the Principles provide a solid framework for a body of wisdom tales, and, although by no means exhaustive, this book touches upon all of the Principles. The Principles are broad enough that I hope story lovers from other faith backgrounds will also find this book useful. The messages range from the value of all life in our interdependent web of being to the importance of kindness, from supporting one another to freedom of thought, from promoting democracy and justice to seeking peace. The stories are organized under these broad categories, as well as others. Each story is also tagged with more specific themes: kindness, integrity, imagination, connection, generosity, justice, hope, and much more. You may find still more themes than I have identified. After all, folktales are many layered and full of wisdom.

Storytelling and Humility

Many readers of this collection will be choosing stories for the lessons they offer. This is tricky business; stories lose their power when presented with too narrow a purpose. As tellers we must trust the intelligence of our listeners and allow them to draw out the wisdom. Humility is important since audiences often relate to and learn from stories in ways we cannot predict and, when listeners find the pearls themselves, they are more likely to remember them. Posing a question within or after a story can help lift up the lesson in a story with less risk of being pedantic or moralizing. To help you and your listeners reflect on their wisdom, I have crafted open-ended questions to go with each story and I encourage you to augment my questions with your own. As acclaimed storyteller Elisa Davy Pearmain says, "Every story is a mystery that may take several keys to unlock." But questions can narrow the meaning of the story and should be used with caution, or not at all. It's important to acknowledge that listeners hear a story in their own special way and may find meaning that the questions don't touch upon. Generally I share my questions only in smaller group settings. Mainly I find the questions useful as a way for me to zero in on the most important aspects of the story while I'm preparing to tell it. This simple reflective act helps bring out the meaning and makes the telling of the story more powerful.

Multicultural Stories Made Personal

As I've continued treasure hunting for stories and reflecting on their lessons, I have been amazed by their universality. In virtually every culture, there are stories that explore the big questions about what it means to be human. The same themes, like humility, courage, kinship, and honesty, pop up in stories from all around the world. Sometimes stories are almost identical except for a change of setting. Other times, a story from another culture can be so different from what we are accustomed to that it can be difficult to discern the message, and we have to be careful not to misconstrue meaning if we don't want to be guilty of cultural misappropriation. Even stories from our own cultures can be a challenge because they push us outside the comfort zone of linear thought. In the Unitarian Universalist tradition of encouraging and accommodating diversity, I have aimed at cultural diversity within this collection and focused particularly on stories that are less commonly found in modern storytelling collections. Hearing a story from another culture is an opportunity to learn about that culture and be reminded that other peoples have much to teach us. But to tell a story from a distant place and time is a challenge because we don't necessarily know whether we are taking the story out of context. I prefer to tell stories from cultures with which I am at least a little familiar, but I've fallen in love with numerous tales from far and wide, and admittedly, I walk a fine line at times. The stories told here are my own interpretations. Overall, I have done all I can not to misconstrue meaning by going back to original sources as much as possible and learning what I can about the culture and geography of the story. I want to be able to see in my mind's eye, so that my listeners can also see, the landscape and architecture of the story's setting. I like to know the foods eaten, the clothes worn, and the currency exchanged. I work hard at imagining the characters and how they think and feel. I try to contextualize so that I know where and why the story is happening. My travels have provided some visceral learning in this regard but, of course, I am limited by my experience and by what I can glean from the stack of books in front of me and the resources available through the Internet. In the introduction to each story, I offer some of the background information and include comments about my interpretations in the cases where I have taken some liberties.

I have done my best to keep the stories lively and true to their spirit. However, in rescripting some of the stories, I've playfully asked "what if?" and "is there another possibility?" For example, in a few cases, such as Ukko's Bread, I've imagined the character learning from their mistake. In other cases, such as The Hole Boy, I've described the main character in a way that I think is more comfortable for audiences today. In doing this, I risk misappropriation, yet I am following a long line of tradition. From the time of Perrault and the Grimm brothers, and the oral tellers long before that, folktales have been changed and manipulated to suit the circumstances of the day, the nature of the audience, and the values of the tellers and their listeners. As Italo Calvino said, "The tale is not beautiful if nothing is added to it." As you begin to prepare a story for telling, you will respond to it in your own way, as has every other teller who has told it. Much as we each have a particular way of revealing moments from our lives, there isn't a right or wrong way to tell a folktale. In fact, each time you tell that story it will be unique and different because you will be responding to the people in the room or the storm raging outside. I believe that the more of ourselves and the present moment that we weave into our stories, the better they are.

Sharing the Stories

One of the best ways to appreciate something beautiful is by sharing it. With this book, I am delighted to be able to offer readers my small harvest of wisdom tales. The more people who are exposed to stories, the more they can serve their teaching purpose. My hope is that many of you will breathe new life into the stories, whether with large audiences, in small group settings, or with your family and friends at home. Seek out their wisdom by repeating them and sharing them with others. You may wish to use the questions that appear after each story to help you prepare to tell them or as a beginning point for conversations or journaling. As you laugh, cry, and have fun with the stories, you will get to know yourself and others better. You may even find that you change, just a little, as I have.

Tips for Telling

WHEN MY FATHER begins to recount a yarn, it is as though we are all there, with him. Perhaps that is why my sister Karen Gummo and I have become performance storytellers. Karen has been at it a little longer than I have, and her advice about how to weave a masterful story is simple and yet profound: "Love your story. Love your audience. Love yourself."

Love Your Story

Let it choose you. Then choose how to tell it.

It's true! Stories that you feel most drawn to are the ones that you will be able to breathe some of yourself into. Whether you identify with the main character, feel puzzled by the chain of events, or relish the messages of the story, your passion for and interest in the story will make your telling shine. Even if you don't understand why you love a story, the ones that draw you in are the best ones for you to tell.

The stories in this collection are written in a way that they can be told. That being said, I encourage you not to worry about memorizing all the words. Instead, think of your story as a house that you're going to show your audience and focus on three main aspects:

- Be very familiar with the entrance and exit, i.e. learn the beginning and end of your story well.
- Use the story text to imagine the different rooms (scenes), but embrace and enjoy the freedom to find your own words in the actual telling.
- Plan out the route you'll follow on a tour of your story house, but know that you can always double back if you forget something along the way.

Imagining the story as a house, or more accurately the blueprint for a house, gives you the freedom to change and grow it in response to the current situation and audience. It brings the story into the present and makes the listeners feel as though they are co-creating it. Audiences relish stories told in this way!

To help you understand my house tour approach, each of the tales in this collection has been pared down to its essential plot line and presented in story map format. In the maps, the scenes from the story are captured by a short description.

If you have time to take your story preparations a step further, you may wish to compare my versions with my source stories. Perhaps that will help you feel greater freedom to breathe something of yourself into the stories and imbue them with your own experiences and insights. When you do, they are bound to grow and flourish.

Make the story your own as you learn it.

Each teller has their own way of learning a story. Here is a more detailed version of the approach that works well for me:

- Begin by choosing a story that you truly enjoy.
- Read it over multiple times, in your head and out loud.
- Draw or jot down the main scenes of the story and check them against the story map from the book.
- Get to know the scenes, and then use your own words to describe each scene as you practice telling the story. *Listeners love it when you inject your own personality and style into the story.*
- Go back to the story text in the book to look for details you may have missed or for lines that you really love.
- Consider your audience and what typically makes them laugh or moves them.
- Augment your story map if needed.

Tell the story again, and again. Pace yourself and vary your pace. *Most of us need to practice slowing down.*

When you are satisfied, find someone with appreciative ears. By this I mean a listener who will promise to listen to you tell the story from start to finish, without interruption, and offer feedback *only* if you ask for it.

I know of tellers who practice in front of the mirror. I prefer to practice a story when out walking, or in front of my kitchen clock. Using a timepiece helps me stay focused and on task while kindly informing me if I've gone on for too long.

There are many inspirational techniques for further enlivening a story. I like to imagine details about the characters and/or setting: what they look like, how they walk and talk, their favorite foods, and more. Please check the references listed at the end of this section for more ideas on workshopping a story.

Love Yourself
Take care of yourself as you tell your story.

- Prepare well, as described above.
- Immediately before telling, take time to breathe in and out slowly several times.
- Use a microphone for large groups.
- Before you begin, look at your audience and smile.
- Trust yourself! Let the story move through you. If you know the scenes, you can tell the story. Even if you forget a scene, you'll find a way to include it.
- Enjoy yourself! Remember that your listeners are on your side and look forward to hearing your story.

Love Your Audience
Help your listeners co-create the story.

An oral story is a presentation, or a true gift to our listeners. When we tell a story effectively we are present to the room, the people who are in it, and to ourselves. We look at our audience, smile, encourage participation, and respond to our listeners' responses.

People have many different ways of enjoying a story; aim to love them all. I've been surprised many times by people whose eyes were closed, or who appeared distracted; over the years, I've found that they have been just as likely to comment on a story as someone who appears to have hung on to every word. People who question a story can be our best teachers, helping us see the story through a new lens.

Participation in a story can range from active listening to laughter, sighs, or tears; repeating an action or refrain; or taking a role in the story. Keep active audience participation opportunities in mind, but keep them optional. Not everyone wants to get actively involved. For me, some of the most enjoyable active participation is spontaneous, or appears to be. For example, I try *not* to use words to get people to join in on making sound effects, repeating a refrain, or singing a song. Instead, I do the action and say or sing the refrain slowly and clearly. Then I repeat it, and nod or smile to the audience, giving them silent permission to join in. I may put my hand to my ear or use my hands and arms like a music conductor. They understand! Be sure to nod and smile when listeners do catch on so they know they aren't disrupting you.

Performance time is often limited, so it's best not to waste much of it organizing the participation while you are telling. Another possible approach is to "plant" audience participation by talking to members of the audience prior to your presentation and coaching them on the sound effect, refrain, or song. Or if you want people to come forward as volunteers, you can ask a few people in advance of your story whether they'd be willing to be the first to step up when you ask for volunteers.

Love Your Audience
Make them laugh.

Not all stories are funny, nor should they be. Even so, a little bit of laughter is an enriching aspect of audience involvement. Stories that seem purely silly can be full of wisdom, and stories that seem purely serious might include humorous details. We can choose humorous stories or inject humor into some stories. Recent studies indicate that laughter releases memory-enhancing hormones. Even a smile has great power to lighten our spirits, which in my mind is a form of enlightenment.

Laughter often arises when something unexpected happens. Here are a few tips for adding humor and helping people recognize it:

- Incorporate what is happening in the room into your story. For example, if you can hear rain on the roof or children are squirming, you might say "and the rain poured down," or "and the children sat very still."
- Use audience member names as positive and likeable characters in the story.
- Weave bits of whatever has just happened into the story. For example, if someone has been talking about a frog or a financial advisor, there might be a way to weave that frog or the financial advisor into the story.
- After you've attempted to be funny, remember to smile so that people know the humor was intentional. If you are moved to laugh—laugh! Give your listeners a moment to laugh before continuing the story.

Love Your Audience

Keep their attention.

If you rework the stories, keep in mind that brevity is a blessing. Try to discern what is most important about the story to help you pare away extraneous details and distractions. You might want to use the reflective questions that appear after each story to help you discern the message that you hope to emphasize in your telling. Ultimately, the most important question to ask yourself when working on a story is "What is the most important thing about the story?"

Love Your Audience, Love Your Story, and Love Yourself

Most of all, aim to have fun and enjoy the process of telling a story. This helps ensure that your listeners will do the same.

Storytelling Resources

Lipman, Doug. *Improving Your Storytelling: Beyond the Basics for All Who Tell Stories in Work and Play*. Little Rock, AR: August House, 1999.

MacDonald, Margaret Read. *The Storyteller's Start-Up Book: Finding, Learning, Performing and Using Folktales*. Little Rock, AR: August House, 1993.

Maguire, Jack. *Creative Storytelling: Choosing, Inventing, and Sharing Tales for Children*. Somerville, MA: Yellow Moon Press, 1991.

Sawyer, Ruth. *The Way of the Storyteller*. New York: Penguin, 1990.

Living with the
Natural World

Children of Darkness

Since trees truly are the lungs of the earth, it feels right to begin a collection of wisdom tales with an excerpt of the Maori creation myth that honors them. In it, the god of forests plays a pivotal role—the gift he offers may surprise you.

IN THE TIME BEFORE TIME, there was nothing. Not a thing!

Who knows how it happened, and whether it was caused by a spark or a shudder or a breath of wind. But suddenly the moon rose, the sun shone, and Papanui (Earth Mother) and Rangi (Sky Father) were revealed.

The attraction between Earth Mother and Sky Father was magnetic. Nothing else existed for them. They fell into an embrace that was so close and went on for so long that they had seventy sons!

They continued to lay in an embrace so close that their children, those boy-gods, dwelt in darkness. They had no room to move or play or grow.

The boy-gods felt suffocated without space and light. They whispered and complained; they plotted and planned. [*You might involve your audience in making sound effects.*]

The god of war shouted, "Let's kill Papanui and Rangi!"

But sixty-nine brothers shouted, "No!" and continued to plot and plan.

Finally, Tane, the god of forests, spoke: "Let us push our mother and father apart!"

Sixty-eight brothers shouted, "Yes!" The god of storms raged in disagreement, but the others ignored him and proceeded with the plan.

The god of edible plants pushed up against the Sky Father with all his might.

He could not budge Rangi.

The god of fern roots and wild berries pushed up against Sky Father with all his might. He could not budge him.

The god of men and women tried and failed.

The god of fish and reptiles was unsuccessful.

And so it went: One god after another was unable to separate Papanui and Rangi. Defeated, they turned to Tane, the god of forests. "It is a good idea, but it is impossible!"

Tane lay down on the ground. He braced himself against Earth Mother and gathered her strength into his shoulders. He lifted his legs and pressed them against Sky Father. He pushed! Tane pushed and pushed with all his might, until suddenly, there was a groan and then there was a snap! [*You might involve your audience in making sound effects.*] Tane had separated his parents.

Tane and sixty-eight of his brothers rejoiced. They leapt and cavorted, celebrating the newfound space and light all around them. [*More sound effects.*]

Sky Father floated high above his wife and was full of sorrow. He cried and continues to cry tears of rain, which make her more beautiful than ever. Earth Mother responds by sending mist skyward.

Meanwhile, the gods busied themselves with their work of creating the world.

Each god did as he was called to do. Tane decorated his mother with trees and plants of all shapes and sizes. He searched out sparks of light and threw them into the heavens to decorate his father with stars.

The god of storms joined his father in upper realms and lives there still. As you well know, he continues to rage—that's how it is with some people.

His rage undoes some of their work, but Tane and the other gods go on creating and tending to Earth Mother and all that dwells there.

To this day, amongst the Maori people and all New Zealanders, Tane is famous for his forests and for his upright strength. Because his feet are rooted in the earth while his head reaches into the sky, he brings together the best of Earth Mother and Sky Father.

FOR REFLECTION

- When have you had enough (or not enough) space and what impact has that had on you?
- To me, it's not surprising that a tree/the god of forests would give the gift of space. What other elements do the same for you?
- When have you been like the god of storms, and the only one to disagree with a plan?
- How might the European utilitarian view of forests have impacted the Maori people who traditionally tell this story?

THEMES

activism, anger, anti-oppression, beauty, birth, calling, change, children, choice, coming of age, creativity, dissent, Earth, environment, family, freedom, God/Goddess, governance, growth, happiness, hope, interdependence, leadership, mystery, nature, parents, power, purpose, self-care, self-respect, strength, teamwork, transformation, vision

PRINCIPLES

- Inherent worth and dignity of every person
- Acceptance of one another and encouragement to spiritual growth
- Right of conscience and use of the democratic process
- World community with peace, liberty, and justice for all
- Respect for the interdependent web of all existence

- All is darkness.
- The moon rises and the sun shines. This reveals Mother Earth and Father Sky.
- They are magnetically attracted! Their close embrace gives rise to seventy sons, all gods.
- They continue to embrace, leaving their sons in darkness, without space.
- The sons plot. The god of war suggests killing their parents. Sixty-nine brothers say "no!"
- The sons plot. The god of forests suggests pushing their parents apart. Sixty-eight say "yes!" (God of storms disagrees.) Sixty-eight ignore the one.
- Several gods try and fail to push their parents apart.
- So it continues until they are ready to give up. Finally the god of forests tries.
- Tane lies on the ground to gather the strength of Mother Earth and pushes.
- He continues to push. There are groans and then SNAP! Mother Earth and Father Sky are separated.
- The sixty-eight brothers celebrate.
- Father Sky cries. His tears make Mother Earth more beautiful. She sends mists rising up to Father Sky.
- Meanwhile, the gods go about their business of creating the world.
- Tane's job is to decorate his mother (with trees and other plants). He gathers sparks of light to decorate Father Sky with stars.
- The god of storms dwells with Father Sky in the heavens and still rages now and then, undoing some of his brothers' work.
- The other gods go on recreating.
- Tane is still famous for bringing together the best of the earth and sky.

The Voice of the Great Spirit

▦ ◆ ▦ ◆ ▦

We all make mistakes! But it is possible to move on. This very old story from the Ngarrindjeri Aboriginals of South Australia encourages us to take time to listen to, respect, and value the interconnected web of all being.

LONG AGO when the world was new, people rose very early in the morning.

It was hard to do, before the sun had begun to warm the earth. But even so, the Aboriginal People of Australia got up early, for it was the time each day when the Great Spirit spoke and shared wisdom.

Even the listening was hard. They could hear the words, but they could not see the Great Spirit. It took great concentration.

People are people.

After a time, one and then another began sleeping late in the morning.

They began to agree that it wasn't necessary to rise so early. They didn't need to hear the Great Spirit every day.

Life was good so long as hunting went well and there was sufficient food. They could make their own *corroboree*—a ceremony with song and dance. They didn't need to get up early.

People are people.

The Great Spirit grieved.

He wanted to give a sign that the people could understand. He asked his servant Narroondarie to gather the tribes one last time.

They came.

Narroondarie motioned for them to find a place around a large gum tree that was growing in the center of the clearing. When all the tribes were seated and silent, there was a loud cracking sound. The gum tree had split wide open.

The people stared. A huge *thalung*, a tongue, had descended from the sky and disappeared into the center of the tree. The tree closed around it.

All were silent. And then, Narroondarie told the people they could return to their hunting and their corroborees. They shrugged their shoulders and away they went.

After a time, some of the people grew bored. Seeking pleasure didn't give them lasting satisfaction. They wanted more from life. They longed to hear the Great Spirit's voice.

They went to Narroondarie for help, but he said, "No. The Great Spirit will not speak to you again."

They went to the graves of their ancestors for help. They asked the Nebulae in the Milky Way for help. Still there was no answer.

They grieved. They painted themselves white with clay. They looked up to the great constellation we call the Southern Cross. They called to Wy young gurrie, the wise old fellow who lives there.

Wy young gurrie invited them to gather around the gum tree once more.

They came. They sat in silence. Wy young gurrie spoke.

He asked, "Did you see the Thalung descend into the tree?"

They all nodded. They had seen that.

"The Thalung is a sign of the Great Spirit's voice. When the Thalung descended into that tree, it was a sign that the voice of the Great Spirit is in all things."

As Wy young gurrie's message slowly sank in, the people's worry-wrinkles began to disappear.

Since that day, life has been richer.

Since that day, the Aboriginal People have come to recognize the Great Spirit's voice in all things.

It is in the wind that whistles and blows.

It is in the crash of thunder and the gentle pitter-patter of raindrops.

It is in the tinkling of bird song and the gurgling of rivers.

The Great Spirit's voice is everywhere. It speaks through the bushes and trees and their many shades of green; it blossoms with flowers; it is in the shimmer of fishes' scales and the sleek movement of animals.

If we listen, what might we hear?

––––––––––––

FOR REFLECTION

- When have you felt awed by something in the natural world? Might it be what is meant by the "Great Spirit's voice"?
- What are some things that make it difficult to experience the "Great Spirit's voice"? And what makes hearing that voice possible? How might the world differ if more of us took time to listen in this way?
- How might the "small still voice within" relate to this story?

THEMES

awe, beauty, belief, community, connection, Earth, environment, faith, God/Goddess, immanence, interdependence, listening, mindfulness, mystery, nature, presence, religion, revelation, reverence, ritual, sacred, spiritual practice, spirituality, tradition, vision, wonder

PRINCIPLES

- Acceptance of one another and encouragement to spiritual growth
- Free and responsible search for truth and meaning
- World community with peace, liberty, and justice for all
- Respect for the interdependent web of all existence

STORY MAP

- It's hard to get up in the morning.
- Yet the Aboriginals get up early to hear the Great Spirit's voice.
- They find it hard to listen to the voice without seeing the Great Spirit.
- They begin to sleep in.
- Eventually they agree they don't need to wake up and see the Great Spirit.
- The Great Spirit grieves and asks them to gather one last time.
- The people gather and see a *thalung* (huge tongue) descend into a gum tree.
- They shrug their shoulders and go home.
- After a time, the people feel empty. They want to hear the Great Spirit's voice again.
- Narroondarie cannot help them.
- The ancestors cannot help them.
- They paint themselves with white clay and call to Wy young gurrie, a wise man who lives in the Southern Cross.
- Wy young gurrie asks the people to gather at the same gum tree.
- He reminds them of the tongue and interprets the Great Spirit's meaning.
- The people understand that the voice of the Great Spirit is in all things.
- Life becomes much richer as they see, hear, taste, and feel the Great Spirit's voice in everything.

The Priest in Paradise

▦ ◆ ▦ ◆ ▦

This short Mexican tale reminds me of my own experiences of being awed by nature. In the version I drew from, Juan understands that an experience of "God's glory" lasts an eternity. In retelling it, I couldn't help but imagine Juan being moved to share his experience with others. It's a story to trigger a conversation about our relationship with nature and the divine.

JUAN SERVED AS THE PRIEST in a small village in the hills of Mexico. Life for his parishioners was hard. They worked long days and, even so, didn't always have enough to eat.

Naturally, when they came to church they loved to hear about paradise—about the beauty and ease of the afterlife. Padre Juan did his best. But the longer he worked in the parish, the more attuned he became to the suffering of the people and the more difficult it was to find the inspiration to describe paradise.

One day when he was putting on his priestly robes, he was thinking out loud. He was so earnest, you might say he was praying.

"If only I could catch even just a glimpse of paradise, my stories and sermons would be more authentic. I would be much better at helping these villagers."

As he walked out the door and headed for the church, he heard the beautiful call of a small songbird. He'd heard it many times before when rushing about his work. But on this day, he stopped.

The song went on and on with its fine rhythm, gorgeous tones, and beautiful melody. The bird was a true maestro! Juan was enraptured. He stared up at the sound, but couldn't find the singer amongst the thick green foliage. Never mind. The song was enough! Juan stood enjoying it for a long while.

When at last he continued walking to the church, something about the path seemed different. And when he arrived at the place where the church should have been, there was only rubble. Juan was mystified. What had happened?

An elderly man came along the path just then. "Buenos Dios!" called Juan. "Where's the church?"

The man rubbed his chin thoughtfully. "The church?" he asked. He pondered some more.

"Oh yes, I remember my grandmother telling me there was a church here when she was a small girl and that the priest disappeared very suddenly."

Juan shook his head in disbelief.

The man continued, "Sometime after the priest disappeared, there was an earthquake and the church tumbled down."

Juan's mouth was now wide open, incredulous.

It was only when he nodded his head in farewell that Juan noticed how tired the man looked.

"Please sir," called Juan. "Come and sit with me."

The two sat quietly together on the rubble and listened while another small bird sang. The man's face began to relax.

FOR REFLECTION

- When does time seem to stretch to infinity for you?
- When has an experience in nature felt like a taste of the divine?
- In what other ways might the priest have helped his parishioners?

THEMES

acceptance, activism, anti-oppression, arrogance, assumptions, awe, beauty, belief, calling, caring, change, community, compassion, contemplation, doubt, empathy, failure, faith, hope, immanence, interdependence, joy, listening, mindfulness, mystery, nature, poverty, presence, purpose, religion, revelation, reverence, sacred, searching, service, simplicity, sorrow, spirituality, suffering, transcendence, vision, wonder, worry

PRINCIPLES

- Justice, equity, and compassion in human relations
- Acceptance of one another and encouragement to spiritual growth
- Free and responsible search for truth and meaning
- Respect for the interdependent web of all existence

STORY MAP

- Juan is the village priest in a poverty-stricken village.
- His parishioners are very poor and love to hear sermons about the paradise of the afterlife.
- At home, Juan prays for inspiration.
- As he walks to the church, he hears a bird singing.
- He stands still enjoying the beauty of it.
- Finally, he continues on the path.
- There is only rubble! He is mystified.
- An old man comes by.
- He remembers his grandmother telling about a priest disappearing and an earthquake later destroying the church.
- Juan is incredulous.
- He notices the old man's fatigue and invites him to sit.
- Together on the rubble, they hear a bird begin to sing.

The Noble Deer

This rich tale lifts up the possibility of forgiveness, the healing power of nature, and the idea that wealth does not always involve gold. Variations are found in the Philippines, England, and beyond; mine is based on an Indian tale.

ACROSS SEVEN VAST SEAS and over seven rugged mountain ranges, there was a magnificent forest.

Its trees were tall and the bush beneath them thick. Here and there, the forest opened to a sparkling pond or a sandy glade.

It was a beautiful place.

What made it extraordinary was a deer who lived there. It was a stag—larger than any that you or I have ever seen, and with perfect glossy brown fur. Its antlers seemed almost as long as its body, and branched more times than I could count.

Stories about the deer spread far and wide. Hunters came from all directions to try to capture the stag. No matter how many arrows they let fly [*you might make the sound effect of an arrow and put your hand to your ear to invite your audience to "shoot" more arrows*], none came close.

Finally, the king learned about the deer. He began to dream of shooting it and mounting its antlers on the palace wall. How grand the room would look! What a testament to his hunting prowess!

No sooner had he entered the forest than he saw the deer grazing peacefully.

He let an arrow fly. [*You might listen for your audience to make the sound effect.*]

But the deer heard the bow's twang and disappeared between the trees.

The king took chase. The king's horse was swift—swifter than those of his servants.

Soon, he had left them all in the dust.

The king was persistent.

He rode deep and deeper into the forest.

Over and again he caught a glimpse of the deer.

Over and again it disappeared. None of the king's many arrows [*you might listen again for your audience to make the sound effect*] hit the mark.

Finally, he arrived in an area where the bush was too thick to continue.

As he looked around, the king realized he had no idea where he was.

Nor could he see the deer.

He was hot, tired, and thirsty.

And he was lost.

He saw the sparkle of water through the trees.

There was no way his horse could get him there, and so he dismounted.

On foot, he pushed his way through the bush.

Finally, there he was, next to the pond.
    He leaned down to drink his fill, and toppled over.

The king struggled to stand up, but once upright, he found that he could not move his feet.
    He was sinking!

The more he tried to free himself, the deeper he sank.
    He was caught in quicksand.

The nearby trees were out of reach. There was nothing he could do!
    He began to cry for help. No one was in sight—or ear shot.

He struggled some more. All he succeeded in doing was sinking still deeper into the sand.

He began to lose hope. If no one came, he was sure to die!

Suddenly a nose poked out of the bush, followed by the entire head and antlers of the very deer whom the king had pursued.

It walked slowly and carefully toward the king, placed its feet on solid ground, and then bowed its head toward the king.

The antlers were within arm's reach.
    The king looked at the deer.
    Its gentle eyes seemed to be saying yes.
    It moved its antlers closer to the king as though inviting him to take hold of them.

The king could hardly believe his good fortune!

He clung onto the antlers. The deer slowly raised its head and pulled the king free.

As soon as he was on solid ground again, the king bowed before the deer.

"You are truly a noble creature. You saved the very one who was determined to kill you! An act such as this deserves a rich reward!"

Even on the hunt the king carried gold.

He searched in his robe for his pouch, but when he offered it to his rescuer, the deer took no notice.

By then, the deer had found a patch of forage and was busily moving from one bush to the next, savoring the crisp and juicy leaves.

At that moment, the king knew that the right reward was to allow the deer to live in peace.

When he returned to the palace, the king decreed that the entire forest would be a sanctuary.

Never again did he hunt for sport.

———————

FOR REFLECTION

- Who in your life has been like the deer in the story?
- What might give a person the strength to be as forgiving and generous as the deer?
- What are some of the ways you've been rewarded when you've been forgiving?
- In what ways have you experienced nature as forgiving?

THEMES

animals, arrogance, change, character, choice, compassion, conscience, courage, dignity, empathy, environment, ethics, forgiveness, freedom, gratitude, greed, integrity, interdependence, justice, kindness, nature, non-violence, power, respect, stewardship, violence

PRINCIPLES

- Inherent worth and dignity of every person
- Justice, equity, and compassion in human relations
- World community with peace, liberty, and justice for all
- Respect for the interdependent web of all existence

STORY MAP

- There is a beautiful forest with a magnificent deer.
- Stories of the deer spread far and wide, but hunters have no luck shooting it.
- The king wants it for a trophy.
- He enters the forest with his hunting party. He sees the deer and shoots. The deer escapes.
- The king chases it madly and leaves his hunting party in the dust.
- Deep in the forest, his arrows miss the deer over and again.
- The king realizes he is lost. He is also tired and thirsty.
- He sees water and must dismount to reach it.
- He gets stuck in quicksand and calls for help, but no one can hear.
- Suddenly, the deer pokes its head through the bush and bows its antlers down to the king.
- The king takes hold and is rescued.
- The king bows to the deer. He offers a reward of gold. The deer is not interested.
- The king realizes the best reward he can offer is to leave the deer in peace.
- He creates a sanctuary in the forest and never hunts again.

The Great Hunter
from Aluk

▤◆▤◆▤

It's hard to imagine staying in one place for very long when our highways are jammed with cars and airports and train stations bustle with travelers. But what if we did? In portraying a character deeply connected to his home, this intriguing Greenland Inuit story offers a unique perspective on belonging and a sense of place.

THE ISLAND OF ALUK, off the southeast coast of Greenland, was home to a great hunter.

What is home? [*You might invite your audience to offer their definitions of home.*] Some says it's sweet, or that it's good to be home and where the heart is.

That is truly how the great hunter from Aluk felt. He loved his island, with its cliffs rising up out of the clear azure sea. He loved it so much that every summer, even when his kinsfolk left Aluk to go hunting in richer waters, he stayed at home.

Every morning, he got up before the sun had risen. He got up and immediately went to the tall cliff rising above the sea, facing to the east. He perched there and waited.

Then suddenly, there it was, that ball of fire on the horizon—its light rays bouncing off the icebergs and painting them yellow then pink, purple then turquoise.

The hunter had an *umiak*, one of the great hunting kayaks that could have easily carried him far to the north with his kinsfolk. Instead, he used it to hunt in the waters around Aluk. Though the waters there weren't as rich in summer as the ones to the north, he was a good hunter and managed to bring in a bounty of fish and seals and walruses.

The hunter remained on Aluk for many long years, first alone with his wife and later with their son.

Their son loved winter. That was when all the other families were at Aluk, living together in the great hall. There were children to play with and there were games, songs, and stories.

All winter long, the boy heard tales about summer travels, and he longed to be able to go. But he knew that his father loved the summers at Aluk, so the boy didn't dare to ask. In late spring, he watched sadly as the other families packed their belongings for the great journey and hunt to the north.

The great hunter fashioned a kayak for the boy so that he could teach him to paddle and hunt.

Like his father, the boy became a great master with his spear and his hooks. With time, he began to hunt alone. As his father aged, he became the family's sole provider.

Supplying his father and mother with food gave the young man courage. Finally one early spring, he decided to ask his father if they could please join the others on the journey north.

The father said nothing. Later that day, the young man asked again. The father shrugged his shoulders and, without smiling, said, "The umiak skin is growing old. Perhaps we'll find a replacement for it in the north."

The young man was ecstatic!

Preparations for the trip didn't burden him in the least.

Before long, they were travelling north with their kinsfolk. Laughter filled the umiaks—except where the father sat.

The journey was as the son had hoped. They met new people; they came to many beautiful bays and coves; they were successful in the hunt.

Meanwhile, the father grew increasingly unhappy. Worst of all for him was that wherever they camped, the sun rose over the mountains instead of out of the sea. He could hardly bear it.

Finally, the father felt he had to return home. The son was sorry, but he was good and faithful and loved his father very much. The next day, they turned their boat toward Aluk.

The days of paddling were long. The father could hardly sleep at night with his deep desire to see the sun rise from the sea. The journey took its toll on him and he grew very weak.

On the last day of their travels, they paddled especially far. By the time they arrived on their home island of Aluk, the old man was exhausted. The son set the tent up along the shore where they were sure to have a good view of the sun rising the next morning. For the first time in many days, the father smiled.

The next day, the son woke to the sound of his father leaving the tent. He watched through the flap as his father found a place to sit.

When the sun had risen and its rays hit the tent, the father uttered a long low moan.

The son hurried out of the tent.

His father was dead!

By the look on his face, the son knew his father had died from the pure joy of seeing the sun rise up out of the sea. He had died from the pure joy of being home.

The son sat on the beach, full of emotion.

He noticed the ball of fire just above the horizon, its rays of light bouncing off the icebergs and painting them yellow then pink, purple then turquoise.

When the time was right, the son dug a grave on the cliff top where his father had loved to watch the sun rise.

Some say that the son chose never to leave his island home again.

Home, where the heart is. [*You might repeat some of your audience's definitions of home.*] Home sweet home.

FOR REFLECTION

- The word *grounded* is used to describe someone who is well balanced and sensible. How important is a sense of place for you in feeling grounded?
- What difference might staying in one place make to how we treat that place?
- What place is especially important to you?
- What is the impact on our lives when we follow our parents' or our children's wishes?

THEMES

acceptance, aging, awe, beauty, belonging, caring, change, children, choice, commitment, compassion, courage, culture, death, depression, despair, dignity, empathy, environment, family, generosity, happiness, identity, interdependence, joy, kindness, love, loyalty, nature, parents, regret, relationships, sacrifice, sense of place, sorrow, suffering, youth

PRINCIPLE

- Justice, equity, and compassion in human relations

- The great hunter's home is the Island of Aluk (Greenland).
- What is home? Where the heart is. Home is sweet and good.
- The hunter loves his home and wants never to leave it.
- He sits atop a cliff every morning, where he loves to watch the sun rise right out of the sea.
- He has an umiak and can travel but doesn't. Instead, he captures all the food he needs in local waters.
- Eventually, he has a son.
- The son loves winter when their kinsfolk live on the island. He enjoys playmates, games, songs, and stories.
- The son loves travel stories and wishes to join the other families when they travel but doesn't dare ask his father.
- The father builds the boy a kayak and teaches him to hunt.
- The son becomes a very skilled hunter. Eventually he becomes the family's provider.
- The son now dares ask his father to go north with the others. The father does not reply.
- The son asks again later in the day.
- The father acknowledges they need new skins for the umiak.
- The boy is ecstatic. Packing feels easy.
- They head north with the others. The boats are full of laughter and song. The father remains quiet.
- The boy loves the new places they see and the people they meet.
- The father is especially disconsolate that the sun rises over the mountains instead of out of the sea.
- The father is so homesick that he must return home. The son agrees.
- They paddle long days toward Aluk. The father can't sleep at night and grows weak.
- On their arrival at Aluk, the father is exhausted. The son sets their tent at a site good for seeing the sunrise.
- In the morning, the father goes out before the son wakes. When the sun hits their tent, the son hears the sound of his father's groan.
- He races outside to find his father lying dead. He has died from the pure joy of being home.
- The son watches the sun rise.
- He buries his father at the cliff-top sunrise outlook.

Baldy

❖❖❖

Imagine if there were magical people to poke and prod us into looking after the land! In my quest for stories that stress the importance of caring for the earth, I was delighted by this whimsical tale from my Scandinavian heritage. My version is an expansion of the brief anecdote I found; it remains true to the original allegorical idea, that when we care for nature and all its magic, it takes care of us. It might be told at a celebration of spring, on Earth Day, or for any event that focuses on environmental stewardship.

LARS WAS A MAN who always had a smile on his face. You'd often hear him say, "I have little money, but I've got lots of time."

It was true. He used his time well. He worked things out and made things work.

It's not surprising that Lars would be the one to take on the challenge of the farm down Nykoebing way. It had changed hands more often than most people changed clothes. No sooner did a family move in than they would find themselves hurrying to leave.

Some folks said it was on account of the soil.

It was too soggy, or too sour, or too shallow to grow a proper crop or pasture animals.

Other folks said the place was haunted.

But Lars paid no heed to any of these stories. He was thrilled that at long last there was a farm he could afford to buy. He emptied every last coin from his pocket to pay for it and gladly took the keys.

It was almost dusk when Lars arrived. Even in the dim light, he could see that the fields and pasture lands were barren and bald. As he walked through the gate, he called out, "Good evening, Baldy!"

To his great surprise, he heard a little wee voice reply, "Hello to you too!" Or was he imagining things? He wasn't sure. Just in case, he called back, "If there is someone here, you are invited to join me for dinner on Christmas Eve."

Lars soon forgot everything about his unusual introduction to the farm. He was too busy!

He repaired the stable to protect his cow, pig, and sheep from the cold.

He patched up the tumbled down fences so the animals could go out to pasture.

He fed and watered the animals.

He harvested the scrawny vegetables.

He plowed the fields and seeded a cover crop.

And then the repairs began again!

There never was a dull moment—one chore or another was always waiting to be done.

By the time Christmas arrived, Lars was ready for a rest and a celebration of his hard work. He roasted the fattest goose he could find, caramelized a few potatoes, and chopped a red cabbage very finely. He was about to sit down to his special meal, when he heard a knock at the door.

He hurried to open it, and looked all around. No one was there. Just in case, he called out, "Good evening, and Happy Christmas to you!"

A wee little voice replied, "I've come for the dinner."

Lars looked more carefully and finally saw a little man—not

much higher than Lars's knees. His nose was hooked. His beard was long and grey. He wore a red jacket, grey striped trousers, black clogs, and a little red hat.

Lars's visitor was not a person but a small and magical elf, called a *nisse* in Danish. And when the nisse pulled off his cap, Lars saw that he was as bald as the land had been.

Soon the two sat together at the table, sharing food. Lars made conversation and joked, a little nervously. Baldy—that was the nisse's name—didn't say much, but he seemed to enjoy himself, smacking his lips. Suddenly, he stood up to leave at the end of the evening, announcing, "On New Year's Eve, I'll serve your dinner to you. Come to the stable."

When the time came, Lars wondered if he'd misunderstood—he couldn't see the little man at the stable. Just in case, he called out, "Happy New Year's Eve to you!"

Baldy emerged from behind a large rock. "This way," was all he said. Lars followed him down a narrow winding tunnel and soon entered a chamber glowing with candlelight. Baldy served salt cod and green leeks—a perfect New Year's meal. Lars eagerly sat at the table.

Just as he was about to take his first bite, Baldy suddenly grabbed Lars's plate right out from under his spoon. Lars was stunned.

Before he could protest, a great big black drop of goo fell from the ceiling to the table exactly where Lars's plate had been.

"Thank you for rescuing my meal!" Lars exclaimed. He moved over to sit up against the wall of the cave beside the nisse. The two ate in silence, watching as more and more dark liquid oozed out of the ceiling and dripped on to the table.

"We've got to do something about this! Perhaps I could patch up the ceiling."

"Won't help," grunted Baldy.

"What's causing the leak? Is there a creek I could divert? Is there a pond nearby?"

"It's your animals."

"My animals?" Suddenly Lars understood that they were directly beneath the stable. The dark liquid was more unpleasant than he'd realized!

"Perhaps I could dig out a new home for you. I could make it bigger if you like. Round, square, whatever shape you want. It could be on the other side of the farmyard."

"No," snarled the nisse. "My home has been here for a thousand years."

"Oh," said Lars, his mind whirring. "You'd like me to move the stable?"

"Indeed."

The very next day, brick by brick, and board by board, Lars began to move the stable all the way over to the other side of the farmyard, as far as possible from Baldy's home. He worked long and hard, until at last he was able to move his animals into their new dwelling.

A month later, Lars began to notice his cow had grown plump, the sheep's wool had thickened up, and his pig had a lovely rosy glow. What's more, that spring every seed he sowed sprouted! Come summer, his rye and oats grew taller and thicker than the grains grown by any of his neighbors.

Folks from far and wide dropped by. They all wanted to know his secret. Lars would only say, "It took time to work things out and make things work."

I'm not sure why, but it was only to me that he spoke of his good friend Baldy.

———

FOR REFLECTION

- What current environmental practices might enrage an elf like Baldy?
- In what ways would the world be different if we adopted Lars's attitude of generosity to the land?
- What are some of the ways we are called to be generous with the land today?
- What significance might there be in Lars "knowing" Baldy's name? When we name something, how does it change our relationship to that thing?

THEMES

caring, conflict, conscience, discernment, Earth, empathy, environment, faith, friendship, generosity, history, hospitality, identity, inclusion, interdependence, justice, kindness, letting go, listening, non-violence, peace, reconciliation, relationships, respect, responsibility, rights, sense of place, stewardship, wealth, work

PRINCIPLES

- Inherent worth and dignity of every person
- Justice, equity, and compassion in human relations
- World community with peace, liberty, and justice for all
- Respect for the interdependent web of all existence

STORY MAP

- Lars is a happy, philosophical person.
- He has the right personality to take over the problem farm.
- Lars doesn't worry that the soil may be poor or that it may be haunted. He is happy to have a farm.
- He arrives at dusk and sees that the land is barren and bald. He calls out, "Hello Baldy."
- He thinks he hears an answer and invites the speaker to Christmas dinner.
- He is soon busy with farm work: repairing the stable and fences, taking care of the animals, harvesting, doing more repairs.
- Christmas comes. He prepares a feast and hears a knock at the door.
- No one is there. Just in case, he calls, "Happy Christmas!"
- A voice replies, "Here for dinner." It's a nisse (Danish elf). Lars sees that he is bald, like the land.

- Lars and the nisse eat together. The nisse is silent but enjoys the meal.

- The nisse invites Lars to New Year's dinner.

- When the time comes, Lars can't see the nisse at the stable. Just in case, he says, "Happy New Year."

- The nisse appears and leads Lars below the stable into his cave.

- He fills Lars's plate. Lars sits at the table. Suddenly the nisse grabs Lars's plate back. Lars is surprised.

- Big drops of black goo land on the table where the plate was. Lars is now grateful.

- Lars and the nisse eat together sitting along the wall of the cave.

- Lars is concerned about the goo and asks the nisse what can be done.

- The nisse is disgruntled: Patching the ceiling won't work, nor does he want a new home. He has lived in the cave for a thousand years.

- Lars understands that he must move the stable.

- Brick by brick, board by board, he moves the stable to the other side of the farm.

- When the stable is moved, the animals become far healthier and the crops are much more abundant.

- When the neighbors ask why, Lars is evasive. He tells only me!

To Whom Does the Land Belong?

❖ ❖ ❖

This story turns land ownership upside-down. From both Muslim and Jewish traditions, it prompts a consideration of our relationship to the places we call home and how we might work together to care for our home.

A FARMER DECIDED TO ADVENTURE to a far-off land. Before he left, he found a man who agreed to look after his property while he was away. The caretaker could grow whatever crops he liked on the land and keep whatever profit he made while the farmer was away.

One year went by. Two years disappeared. Ten years flew past. Finally, twenty years later, the landowner returned.

When he arrived home, he could immediately see that the caretaker had done an excellent job. The fields were green and lush. Fruit hung heavy on the branches of the trees. He could hear the bleats and clucks of contented animals in the stable. The farm couldn't have been in better shape.

When the caretaker recognized that the visitor was the farmer who'd left so long ago, he invited him in for tea. The two men exchanged news and gossip, and the farmer thanked the caretaker heartily. As their conversation was drawing to a close, the farmer asked, "Where will you go now?"

"Go?" said the man, "Where should I go? After all these years of care and labor, surely the land belongs to me!"

The farmer was perplexed. "How could it possibly belong to you? It's mine and always has been!"

The two men argued for a long time. Finally, the only thing they could agree on was to take their dispute to the wise man in the local village.

The wise man listened carefully to each of their arguments. He was puzzled by the case.

[*You might ask the audience what they think.*]

After a while, the wise man said, "I say we consult a higher authority."

The farmer and caretaker wondered who that might be. Would they need to travel to the city and take their case before the court?

The wise man shook his head. He walked back to the farm with the two men. When they arrived, the wise man lay down on the ground and placed his ear next to the earth.

The farmer and the caretaker watched. The wise man lay there for a long time.

Finally he stood up, brushed off his robe, and declared, "The land belongs to neither of you."

"What?" cried the two men together.

"The land has told me that you both belong to it."

The wise man bowed his head in farewell, then turned back home.

The two men looked at one another for a long time.

FOR REFLECTION

- What advice might the land give to the two farmers?
- How might the farmers begin to get along?
- What might the land tell us today?

- How would it be different to "belong to" rather than "own" the land?
- How might "belonging" help resolve conflicts over territory?
- How might "belonging" change our environmental practices?

THEMES

anger, arrogance, assumptions, authority, belonging, conflict, Earth, environment, ethics, greed, humility, interdependence, letting go, listening, peace, power, reconciliation, relationships, responsibility, rights, sense of place, stewardship, work

PRINCIPLES

- World community with peace, liberty, and justice for all
- Respect for the interdependent web of all existence

STORY MAP

- A farmer heads off on an adventure.
- A caretaker will tend the land. He can take the profits in the farmer's absence.
- One, two, ten, twenty years go by. The farmer returns.
- He is impressed by the good health of the farm.
- The caretaker offers tea. The two men have a friendly exchange until the farmer asks the caretaker, "Where will you go now?"
- The caretaker argues that the land now belongs to him.
- The farmer is adamant that it belongs to him.
- The two argue incessantly.
- Finally they agree to consult with a wise man.
- The wise man listens carefully and is perplexed.
- He says he must consult a higher authority.
- The two men are puzzled when the wise man puts his ear to the ground.
- The wise man listens a long while and then says, "The land says it doesn't belong to either of you. You both belong to it."
- The two men are perplexed, but remain together on the farm.
- Perhaps they begin to listen to the land.

Living with
Ourselves

The Hole Boy

Stories of half-people or half-animals are told in Spain, India, the Middle East, and North America, and by the Tempasuk Dusuns of North Borneo. The latter group's tale of "Half Boy" is full of suffering and joy and conveys the universal message of our need to feel whole. I have felt deeply moved by this story but cautious about the negative association between physical "half-ness" and a lack of psychological wholeness. To make the tale more surreal and more certain to be received as metaphorical, I've imagined the needy boy to be "full of holes."

LONG AGO AND FAR AWAY, and yet not so long ago nor far away, there was a boy.

He was an ordinary boy in every way, except that he felt as though he were full of holes.

He felt as though he had holes everywhere: in his heart, in his head, in his arms, in his legs.

He felt as though he had as many holes as he had body, and he called himself "Hole Boy," beginning with an h.

This feeling of being full of holes made the boy sad and mad all at once.

It stirred up trouble inside him, and so he caused trouble all around him.

When the fishers were preparing to set their lines, Hole Boy tangled them.

When the farmers were planting their fields, Hole Boy raced through and trampled the ground.

When the musicians were preparing to play, Hole Boy shouted and stomped and screamed as loudly as he could.

When the other children were trying to play, Hole Boy found a way to get in their way.

The older Hole Boy grew, the more trouble he caused. People soon had enough, and they let him know!

Children began to jeer and throw sticks at him.

Women called him a pest and shooed him away.

Men scolded him and chased him off.

Finally, it was unbearable to have him around. He could hardly bear himself.

Some people wanted to drive him out of the village; others wanted to destroy him.

But there was one woman who had watched the boy, and she noticed that the trouble was as much inside him as it was outside.

She had compassion for the boy and believed he could change.

She said, "You say you are full of holes and you call yourself Hole Boy. You cause trouble, but I think it is this feeling of holes that causes your bad behavior. If you could feel whole, with a w, everything could change."

The woman continued, "If you venture out into the world, I think you will find the part of you that is missing. I think you will find a boy who also has holes. That boy will make you whole. You will become Whole Boy—with a w. Then you will find your goodness."

The woman's words were puzzling, and yet they were like sweet nectar to the boy.

Never before had anyone had faith in him or shown him such kindness. For the first time ever, he felt warmth in his holey heart. For the first time ever, he had hope.

The next morning, Hole Boy set off. His steps were hesitant and uneven, but he made his way along through thick bush and past giant trees.

[*You might involve your audience in making sound effects whenever the following refrain is repeated.*]

Wind whistled through his holes and blew him about.
Branches snagged him and stopped him short.
Vines grabbed him. Animal sounds frightened him.
The river roared right at him; its spray splashed and soaked him.
But on he journeyed.

Finally at nightfall, he crept into a village square, and asked the people, "Have you seen a boy like me, who is full of holes?"

They pondered for a while.

Finally an old woman said, "We have heard of one like that, somewhere toward sunset."

The next morning Hole Boy set out again and now he made his way for two days through thick bush and past giant trees. [*Sound effects.*]

Wind whistled through his holes and blew him about.
Branches snagged him and stopped him short.
Vines grabbed him. Animal sounds frightened him.
The river roared right at him; its spray splashed and soaked him.
But on he journeyed.

Finally, he came to the next village. When he asked about another Hole Boy, they too pointed toward the sunset.

The next morning, Hole Boy set out again and now he stumbled and bumbled for three days through thick bush and past giant trees. [*Sound effects.*]

Wind whistled through his holes and blew him about.

Branches snagged him and stopped him short.

Vines grabbed him. Animal sounds frightened him.

The river roared right at him; its spray splashed and soaked him.

But on he journeyed.

On the third day, as he approached a third village, he heard a loud cry, "Another Holy Boy! Another Holy Boy has arrived!"

Before long, Hole Boy saw the other boy, the Holy Boy, coming toward him.

There could be no doubt that it was his other half!

The two boys were the same size.

They were each complete in precisely the places where the other had holes.

No one knows why, but that's the way they were.

The boys recognized themselves in one another.

Even so, they weren't quite sure what to make of each other.

They circled around one another, sometimes smiling, sometimes suspicious.

They began to wrestle.

They tussled and tossed and swung one another round.

They stirred up the dust and the dirt and the water in the river.

The wind began to howl, rain pelted down, thunder roared, and lightning flashed.

The boys fought all through the night.

The storm raged all night long.

At last, the sun rose.

All was quiet except for the birds, who sang more beautifully than ever before.

In the calm of morning, a single boy walked out of the river and out of the forest.

He was a Whole Boy now. A Whole Boy (with a w) and without a single hole—except, of course, for the ones that we all have.

Whole Boy said goodbye to the people of the village and made his way back through the forest.

[*You might want to emphasize the calm,
by putting your finger over your lips.*]

Not once did the wind blow him about. Not once did a branch snag him. No vine tripped him. No animal sounds frightened him. Even the river was calm.

When at last Whole Boy arrived in the village where Hole Boy had begun the journey, he found the woman who had believed in him.

She welcomed him home with her arms wide open.

Whole Boy laughed.

That night they feasted, sang, and danced in celebration of his wholeness.

———

FOR REFLECTION

- When has another person's faith in you made a difference to how you behaved?
- When have you believed in someone when others did not? How did you maintain that belief and what difference did it make?
- How do your challenges relate to Hole Boy's struggle on his journey?
- How do your challenges relate to the struggle between the two boys? What kind of struggle do you experience when you strive for greater wholeness (or integrity) in your life?

THEMES

acceptance, anger, brokenness, caring, character, coming of age, community, compassion, conflict, courage, depression, despair, empathy, friendship, growth, happiness, hope, identity, inclusion, journey, kindness, limitations, love, mentorship, relationships, searching, self-acceptance, self-respect, shame, suffering, trust, vulnerability, wholeness, worth, youth

PRINCIPLES

- Inherent worth and dignity of every person
- Justice, equity, and compassion in human relations
- Acceptance of one another and encouragement to spiritual growth

STORY MAP

- A boy feels like he is full of holes.
- He feels holes everywhere, and they make him feel mad and sad.
- The trouble inside him causes him to make trouble around him— with fishers, farmers, musicians, and other children.
- The older he grows, the more trouble he causes.
- People begin to shun him. He shuns himself.
- One woman has compassion and encourages him to journey in search of someone full of holes like himself.
- The boy is puzzled, yet he feels hope for the first time ever.
- The boy's journey is challenging: wind, branches, vines, animal sounds, river.
- At the first village, the boy is sent further. The journey remains challenging.

- At the second village, the boy is sent further. The journey remains challenging.
- At the third village, people see him for who he is.
- The Hole Boy and the Holy Boy recognize one another. They are attracted yet suspicious.
- They begin to wrestle, stirring up dust and stirring up a storm.
- The storm and their fight continue all night.
- At sunrise, all is calm. Then a whole boy emerges.
- The journey home is calm and easy.
- The woman recognizes him.
- They feast to celebrate the boy's wholeness.

Vasilisa, the Brave

Remembering the experience of being loved can help a person find light and hope even in the darkest of places. I've abbreviated this well-known Russian coming-of-age tale to emphasize Vasilisa's ritual and the important role it plays in helping her find the strength to overcome obstacles.

LONG AGO AND FAR AWAY there was a girl called Vasilisa. Sometimes she was called Vasilisa the wise or Vasilisa the brave. She was never called Vasilisa the sad, even though her mother died when she was just eight years old.

Of course she was sad about her mother's passing. But she had fond memories of her too.

Before she died, Vasilisa's mother called her daughter to her bedside and placed a little doll into Vasilisa's hands. It was one she had carved especially for her. Vasilisa's mother said, "Take good care of this little doll, and she will take good care of you."

Vasilisa put the little doll in her pocket. On the day her mother died, despite her tears she remembered to care for the doll. She saved a few crumbs of cake that day and, in the evening, brought them to bed with her, along with a glass of tea. She placed her doll on her pillow, gave her the treat, and a sip of tea. She told the doll her troubles, ending with a question, "Little doll, little doll, what shall I do?"

It seemed that the little doll's eyes shone like fireflies. It was as though she spoke and said, just as her mother had always said, "Do not be afraid, Vasilisa. Be comforted. Say thy prayers and go to sleep. The morning is wiser than the evening."

And it was as true for Vasilisa as it is for me. Things never seem as bad in the morning as they do in the evening.

Every day, Vasilisa would save some bread or a few raisins and bring them, with a glass of tea, to her bed. There she fed her doll and told her all her troubles, ending with the question, "Little doll, little doll, what shall I do?" [*You might want to invite your audience to help with this refrain.*]

Talking to the doll like this always comforted Vasilisa and gave her courage.

Even when her father found a new mother for her, who wasn't her mother!

Even when this woman gave her the worst of all the chores.

Even when this woman sent her to fetch a new flame for their fire and Vasilisa had to walk all alone through the forest, with its creaking trees and dark shadows.

Vasilisa held tight to her little doll and found strength.

Even when she arrived in the forest clearing, at Baba Yaga's hut, which stood on chicken legs and was surrounded by a fence made of skulls and bones.

Even when the horrid Baba Yaga appeared, cackling, spitting, and scary as can be.

Even when the horrid Baba Yaga told Vasilisa that if she wanted the flame her stepmother had sent her to fetch, she must do endless chores: cleaning the whole house and the yard and making dinner too.

Even when the horrid Baba Yaga demanded that, on top of the usual sorts of chores, Vasilisa do impossible things like sorting the chaff from the wheat and the dirt from the poppy seeds.

When Baba Yaga left her alone, Vasilisa cared for her little doll, told her all her troubles, and said, "Little doll, little doll, what shall I do?" [*Audience can say it with you.*]

The little doll reminded Vasalisa not to be afraid and that the morning is wiser than the evening. It was true—the chores did get done!

Baba Yaga was unhappy that Vasilisa managed to do all the impossible tasks! Yet Baba Yaga kept her promises and gave Vasilisa the flame her stepmother wanted. She was only too eager to do so, for she could tell that Vasilisa's strength came from her mother's blessing and this was not something that Baba Yaga liked to be near.

When Vasilisa left, she carried the new flame with her. It allowed her to see the forest with new eyes. She realized it was not dangerous and she was no longer afraid.

When she came to the other side of the forest, she saw, by that same light, that her stepmother's house was not Vasilisa's home and never could be. She walked right past it.

She walked on and on until, at last, she came to the home of another woman, one who welcomed Vasilisa to live with her. This woman encouraged her to care for her doll and taught her the skills needed to find fortune and happiness.

Still, every day, Vasilisa saved some bread or a few raisins and brought them, with a glass of tea, to her bed. There she fed her doll. Now she had as many joys as she had troubles to whisper to the doll.

This story may seem strange. It may not seem true.

The part I believe is that Vasilisa's little ritual helped her.

EXTENSION   You might lead from the story into a ritual—perhaps lighting a chalice or candle, or some other ritual that feels appropriate.

FOR REFLECTION

- How is lighting the chalice (or another ritual) like Vasilisa's care of her doll?
- What are some of your personal rituals that have helped you through challenges?
- When has darkness been your teacher?

THEMES

caring, coming of age, courage, faith, family, fear, growth, hope, love, oppression, parents, relationships, responsibility, ritual, self-care, self-respect, spiritual practice, spirituality, strength, success, suffering, trust, work, worry, youth

PRINCIPLES

- Acceptance of one another and encouragement to spiritual growth
- A free and responsible search for truth and meaning

STORY MAP

- Vasilisa lives on the edge of the forest.
- She is called Vasilisa the brave and Vasilisa the wise, but never Vasilisa the sad.
- She has happy memories of her mother and a special doll made by her mother.
- When her mother dies, Vasilisa gives the doll tea and a treat and asks the doll's advice.
- The doll comforts Vasilisa by reminding her not to be afraid and that things always seem better in the morning than in the evening.

- Sharing tea and a treat and talking with the doll becomes a daily routine for Vasilisa.
- The doll comforts Vasalisa even when her father remarries and her stepmother is unkind. Even when her stepmother sends Vasilisa alone into the forest to find a flame to relight the fire.
- The doll gives Vasilisa strength even when Vasilisa encounters Baba Yaga's frightening hut and Baba Yaga demands that Vasilisa do impossible chores.
- The doll always reminds Vasilisa not to be afraid and helps Vasilisa with chores.
- Baba Yaga is frightening, but honest. She rewards Vasilisa for completing the chores.
- Vasilisa returns to the village with new confidence and courage.
- Vasilisa walks past the home of her stepmother.
- She finds another woman to live with and learn from.
- The story is strange yet true. Rituals like Vasilisa's can help us.

Crow and Partridge

As difficult as it can sometimes be, self-acceptance is one of the ingredients necessary for developing friendships and leading a happy life. This Panchantantra tale from India warns about the folly of imitating others.

I'VE GOT A VERY SAD STORY for you.

Crow sat perched in a tree, surveying the world around him. A Partridge crossed the path below. Crow watched for a while and thought, "What a beautiful way of walking that Partridge has!" For a few moments he sat mesmerized.

Is there a Partridge around here?

[*Continue "looking for a partridge" and smiling until someone volunteers. Encourage them to walk.*]

Crow noticed that Partridge took tiny steps. He moved his feet quickly and delicately.

Crow flew down.

Is there a Crow here?

[*Continue "looking for a crow" and smiling until someone volunteers.*]

Crow landed a little ways behind Partridge. He began to follow along behind Partridge and tried for a very long time to walk just the way that Partridge walked.

It was difficult. Crow's feet were much larger than Partridge's. When he tried to take quick, tiny steps, he tripped over his own toes.

[Thank the volunteers and continue the story.]

Finally, Partridge turned around and asked, "Crow, what are you doing?"

"Don't be angry with me," replied Crow. "I have never seen a bird that walks as beautifully as you. I'm trying to learn to walk like you."

Partridge puffed a little with pride, but then he looked at crow.

"Wait a minute," he said. "I think you are being foolish! You are a crow, and should walk like a crow. You look silly when you try to strut like me."

Crow heard Partridge's words but paid no attention to them. He thought he'd be a better bird if only he could move the way Partridge moved. He went on trying to learn. He tried for so long that eventually he forgot how crows are meant to walk, and he never mastered Partridge's walk either.

Isn't that sad? Poor Crow never realized how lovely a bird he was. Poor Crow never realized he was most beautiful when he was himself.

FOR REFLECTION

- When is it most difficult to be yourself?
- What are some of the things that help you live with authenticity?
- How does accepting and celebrating yourself make it easier also to be with others?

THEMES

authenticity, belonging, culture, dignity, diversity, equality, failure, friendship, growth, happiness, identity, individualism, limitations, mentorship, multiculturalism, purpose, race/ethnicity, relationships, respect, self-acceptance, self-respect, sorrow, success, wholeness, worth

PRINCIPLES

- Inherent worth and dignity of every person
- Acceptance of one another and encouragement to spiritual growth
- Free and responsible search for truth and meaning

STORY MAP

- This is a sad story.
- Crow sits in a tree, watching and admiring Partridge.
- Partridge takes tiny, delicate steps.
- Crow walks behind Partridge and tries to copy him.
- It is difficult! Crow trips over his toes.
- Partridge asks Crow, "What are you doing?"
- Crow admits he is imitating him.
- Partridge is momentarily flattered, but then questions Crow.
- Partridge advises Crow "to be Crow."
- Crow doesn't listen and keeps trying to be like Partridge.
- Crow tries to be like Partridge for so long that he forgets how to be Crow.
- How sad!

The Happy Man's Shirt

Most of us want nothing more than for our children to be happy. This Italian tale calls to mind the most important elements in our quest for joy. Similar stories are told in the Middle Eastern folk tradition and by Hans Christian Andersen and Leo Tolstoy.

ONCE THERE WAS A PRINCE who never smiled.

Never.

The king, of course, desperately wanted his son to be happy.

He tried everything. But the court jester was a bore. Royal balls were intolerable. Princesses were insufferable. The prince spent his days staring listlessly out the window and could not say what ailed him.

The king called for doctors, philosophers, and sages.

After conferring together for countless hours, they came up with the perfect solution.

"You must find a happy man and bring his shirt to your son. Then," they added, "all the happiness of the shirt will envelop and nourish your son."

The idea was unusual, but simple. Why not try? And so the king sent his ambassadors to find a truly happy man.

They came upon a merchant content with his grand home and beautiful family. He seemed just right—until they asked whether he would like to be knighted. His eyes filled with such desperate longing that they knew he was not the man they sought.

They came upon a priest, full of energy and idealism. He seemed just right—until they asked whether he might like to be bishop. He replied, "Nothing would please me more," and they knew this man wasn't perfectly content either.

They traveled far and wide, but wherever they went, no one was perfectly happy. There was always something in the way.

People had:

Too many children, or too few.

Too much work, or not enough.

[You might ask the audience for other ideas.]

Indeed, it seemed that people were either too lonely or overwhelmed by too much company.

They were too hungry, or too full.

They were overtired, or they overslept.

They were never satisfied.

The ambassadors were about to give up when they heard someone whistling a merry tune off in the distance. They followed that melody to its source and found a farmer contentedly weeding.

As they approached, he welcomed them and said with delight, "I could use a break. Please join me for water and fresh picked carrots!"

The ambassadors were accustomed to wine and cake, but they tried the humble offering and found it both refreshing and delicious.

The farmer beamed, "What a glorious day it is! A man couldn't wish for more!"

"Wouldn't a bigger farm be better?"

"A bigger farm would be too much work. Mine is the perfect size!"

"Wouldn't life be easier if you were a merchant or a tradesman?"

"But I'd miss working the soil and breathing the fresh country air."

"But you labor so hard."

"My wife and children help—company makes the work go faster."

"Isn't there anything you wish for?"

After the man had thought hard, he replied, "Nothing!"

The ambassadors were truly perplexed by this very poor but very happy man. They were also thrilled, "You are the man we've been looking for! We have been asked to bring the shirt of a truly happy man to the king."

The man stared at them for a moment. And then laughed apologetically, "But I don't own a shirt."

It was true.

The ambassadors returned to the king empty-handed, but not empty-headed. They knew the prince would need to weave his own shirt of happiness. And they had some ideas for how he might do that.

———————

FOR REFLECTION

- What are some ideas for finding happiness that the king's men might bring back to the palace? How would you suggest the prince weave himself a "shirt of happiness"?
- What are some of the things in life that make you happiest?
- In what ways might getting rid of our "shirts" (or some other luxury) help us to be happy?

THEMES

acceptance, choice, class, depression, dignity, discernment, freedom, gratitude, greed, happiness, hope, humility, joy, letting go, mindfulness, money, pride, privilege, reverence, searching, self-acceptance, self-respect, simplicity, sorrow, success, vision, wealth, wholeness, work, worth

PRINCIPLES

- Inherent worth and dignity of every person
- Acceptance of one another and encouragement to spiritual growth
- Free and responsible search for truth and meaning

STORY MAP

- The prince never smiles.
- The king tries everything from jesters to parties to princesses, but nothing helps.
- The king consults doctors, sages, and philosophers. All agree that the prince needs to wear a happy man's shirt.
- The king sends ambassadors to find a happy man and ask for his shirt.
- A merchant seems happy, but the ambassadors soon realize he's still ambitious.
- A priest seems happy, but the ambassadors soon realize that he, too, is still ambitious.
- Everyone they encounter wants something different or more than they have.
- The ambassadors hear someone whistling. They follow the sound and come to a poor farmer.
- The ambassadors question the farmer; surely he wishes for more wealth, or greater ease, etc.
- No, the farmer is happy. The ambassadors are perplexed but delighted to have found a happy man.
- They ask for his shirt and learn that he doesn't have one!
- They realize that the prince needs to weave his own shirt of happiness and they return with a few ideas about how to do so.

Granny's Ride

When we think of heroes, we often imagine someone who is young, strong, and possibly wearing a cape. In this story from England, our hero knits, is not exactly young, and seems oblivious to her courage and its impact. Granny is an inspiration to me in the way that her story reminds us that we must get on our horse and go, follow our hearts, and stay grounded—even when the unexpected happens.

It all began with a mistake—or so it seemed.

Granny got up out of bed at midnight thinking it was morning and time to be on her way. She was going to Crowcombe market, where she sold her wares every week.

She had a bite to eat and a sip to drink and offered the same to Smart, her old gray pony. He'd been her faithful companion for close to forty years.

She saddled up Smart and attached her pannier to the side. It was a special sort of basket that she loaded up with the breads, jams, eggs, and such that she hoped to sell. She carefully placed her needles and yarn at its very top, so that she could continue knitting her stockings along the journey.

Granny mounted and clicked for Smart to set off. He knew the way well, even in the pitch black of night, and he plodded along in his usual slow manner. Before long, the pony's rhythmic sway sent Granny drifting back to sleep.

She didn't know how long she'd slept nor where they were when Smart stopped. He stood stock still, except that he was trembling all over. She could feel that his mane and tail were stiff with fright.

And then she heard it herself—a gallop of horse's hooves, coming closer and closer. There was something ominous about the sound. She knew it was no ordinary horse and rider.

All of a sudden, a hare jumped out of nowhere right up onto the old horse's back and into the good woman's lap. It too shivered with fright. Granny lifted the lid on her basket and pushed the rabbit inside before replacing the lid.

Her heart was pounding. Her palms were sweating. Then she noticed that Smart was looking down, absorbed in the grass in front of him as though it had some sweetness to it. She knew it didn't. Seeing his focus reminded her that she must stay calm. She reached back into her basket to pull out her needles, and then carefully closed the lid to hide the hare.

Clickety-click. She began to knit.

Clickety-click. She continued to knit.

Clickety-click.

All at once the rider was beside her, in a shadow so dark she could barely see him or his horse. Without so much as a hello, he demanded, "Have you seen a hare run past?"

Clickety-click. Granny didn't look up from her knitting.

Clickety-click. She didn't utter a word, but there was no mistaking by the shake of her head that she was saying no.

And if you think she was lying, she wasn't! The rabbit had not gone past her, it was still in her basket!

But the rider didn't know that. He dug his heels into his horse and galloped away.

Smart, who had done nothing but amble slowly for the last twenty years, suddenly cantered off in the opposite direction. When they reached Roebuck Stream, he hurried down the middle of that stream and didn't let up until the strange hoof beats were long gone.

Such a relief!

A moment or two later, Granny felt a rustle in the basket. She looked down and, to her great surprise, saw a young woman climbing out of it.

"Thank you! Thank you!" repeated the young woman over and again.

Granny patted Smart on his back as she shrugged her shoulders humbly. "We carried on, that's all we did."

"And you saved me!" The young woman's smile lit up like sunshine. Then she explained, "I was bewitched and transformed into a hare. A hare that was destined to be hunted forever, unless I could get behind my pursuers. When you hid me, you saved me! I can never thank you enough."

Granny shrugged her shoulders again. The young woman kissed Granny on her cheek. Then she was gone.

Granny watched a while, as best she could in the dark. Then she and Smart set off again, plodding all the way into Crowcombe.

When they got there, the clock tower told her it was three in the morning. Three in the morning? Granny wondered how she could have made such a mistake with the time. Or was it a mistake? She smiled as she thought of the young woman set free.

Granny lay down on a bench and, before you know it, she was fast asleep, snoring gently. Smart slept standing beside her.

Who'd have known that a horse and a pair of knitting needles could help someone to be so courageous? Then again, some say that the key to finding courage is to relax and trust our hearts to guide us even when we don't think we know what to do.

FOR REFLECTION

- When have you made a "mistake" that proved to be the right thing to do?
- Who or what is the horse that steadies you in your life?
- What might it mean to "get behind your pursuer"?

THEMES

acceptance, activism, aging, caring, choice, compassion, courage, fear, intuition, kindness, purpose, self-respect, success

PRINCIPLES

- Inherent worth and dignity of every person
- Acceptance of one another and encouragement to spiritual growth

STORY MAP

- Granny makes a mistake and gets up way too early not realizing the time.
- She eats and feeds her faithful horse Smart.
- She saddles Smart and loads the pannier with market goods and her knitting.
- They set off in the pitch black. Soon, Granny falls asleep.
- She suddenly wakes and finds Smart shivering with fright.
- She hears a rider coming fast and knows it's no ordinary horse or rider.
- Suddenly, a hare jumps into Granny's lap. It is also shivering with fright.
- Granny hides the hare in her pannier.
- Granny is frightened, but follows Smart's example of pretending not to be.
- She begins knitting.
- The rider appears alongside them and demands to know whether Granny has seen a hare go by.
- Granny says, "No hare has gone by" (it's true!). The rider gallops off.
- Smart hurries into and along the stream bed. For the first time in twenty years, Smart gallops.
- He doesn't stop until it feels safe.
- The pannier begins to move. A girl emerges from it and thanks Granny.
- Granny is mystified.
- The girl explains that she was bewitched and had to get behind her pursuer to become her true self again.
- The girl kisses Granny and leaves.

- Granny and Smart continue to the village. Granny is surprised that it's only three in the morning.
- She realizes she made a mistake. But maybe it wasn't a mistake.
- Granny sleeps on the bench in the village square; Smart sleeps standing beside her.

Trustworthy Traveler

Almost a thousand years ago, Abdul Qadir Jilani was born in a small village in the area we now call Iraq. He was known and loved for his great wisdom, kindness, and integrity. I've been inspired by his intelligence and his commitment to "walk his talk," and imagined some of the details of his early days. He remains an admirable role model for us all.

ABDUL QADIR WAS BORN in a small village long ago. His mother loved her sweet little baby, with his great big eyes. When he was old enough to play, she sent him outside with the other children. He loved watching them. Sometimes they would play games a little like tag or hide and seek. Other times, they would make wheels out of bent sticks and use other sticks to roll them along the sandy streets of town.

Abdul rarely joined in their games.

Mostly, he liked to watch and wonder. Perhaps he wondered:

How many grains of sand are there in the desert?

How far away is the sun?

How many turns of the wheel make a cubit?

Questions, questions, questions.

[*You might want to ask your audience what other questions they suppose he asked.*]

His mother brought him to one scholar and then another so that his insatiable curiosity might be satisfied. He learned arithmetic and geometry from one, calligraphy and poetry from another, and philosophy and ethics from a third. Still, Abdul Qadir remained curious, and full of a longing to learn. If only he could go to Baghdad and study there at the university.

But Baghdad was far away. His father had died and neither he nor his mother relished the thought of him going so far from home. Besides that, they were poor people. Even though university tuition was free in those days in Baghdad, to travel there was expensive—and dangerous —with many thieves along the road. The only safe way to travel would be to hire a camel and join a caravan. This would cost far more money than they had. Abdul didn't feel he could ask his mother for such an indulgence, and so he put his dream aside.

Abdul's mother was relieved, and yet she didn't feel quite right about this. She knew how gifted and good her son was. She thought that if he could study and learn more, a good boy like Abdul would be even more capable of making the world a better place.

She took on as much needlework and washing for others as she could manage. She scrimped and she saved. Eventually she had enough money to arrange for Abdul to join a camel caravan traveling to Baghdad. She made the required payment and carefully sewed the remaining forty silver dinars into his coat. It would be safe there.

Abdul's mother kissed him on his forehead and offered a few words of wisdom: "Remember my son, you must always be kind to others, and you must always be honest. Then you will live a good life." Abdul bowed in agreement and gratitude before he left.

Sitting astride a camel was a new and exciting adventure! Abdul began to wonder:

How many camel strides makes a cubit and how many cubits is it to Baghdad?

How can mountains rise out of the desert?

Why does the moon change its shape?

Questions, questions, questions.

[*You might want to ask your audience what other questions they suppose he asked.*]

On the third or fourth day of their journey, a band of thieves ambushed the caravan. They grabbed jewelry and reached into the travelers' pockets and purses to steal all their coins. Abdul had no purse and the bandits found nothing in his pockets. The thieves had many silver coins, but still they were not satisfied.

Brandishing their scimitars they demanded, "Anyone with more jewels, riches, or dinars, speak now!"

The entire caravan was quiet.

Abdul calmly stepped forward and stated, "I have forty dinars."

The thieves looked at the skinny boy with his homespun coat. "You?" they laughed. They checked his pockets anyway then laughed again, "You wish you had riches!"

Abdul solemnly took off his coat and showed the thieves where the coins were hidden. They stared at him in amazement. One of the thieves began to try to tear the coins from the coat, but the second thief stopped him. He held the coat up in front of Abdul and said, "We would never have known there were coins hidden here. Why did you tell us?"

"I am a boy who keeps his promises. And I promised my mother that I would always be honest."

The thief turned to his companion and the two whispered together with great urgency.

Finally, without a word to the travelers, the second thief placed Abdul's coat on the ground. The first thief poured all the coins and jewels and riches stolen from the members of the caravan onto the coat. The two men then turned on their heels and left.

Abdul quietly returned the coins to their rightful owners.

Soon enough, they remounted their camels and continued the journey to Baghdad. There, Abdul enrolled in university, where he studied for many years. Eventually, he became an imam, a great scholar and teacher. People tell stories about him to this day.

As for the thieves, they were so inspired by Abdul's honesty and courage, they gave up their thieving ways and began to work for the good of all.

As for his mother, I like to think that her son visited her often.

FOR REFLECTION

- When has being honest worked in your favor, even when it seemed to be the foolish thing to do?
- Who or what has given you courage to be honest?
- When have you noticed honesty to be infectious?

THEMES

authenticity, calling, character, children, choice, coming of age, commitment, conscience, courage, dignity, education, ethics, family, honesty, integrity, letting go, money, non-violence, parents, purpose, respect, responsibility, self-respect, strength, success, youth

PRINCIPLES

- Acceptance of one another and encouragement to spiritual growth
- Right of conscience and use of the democratic process

STORY MAP

- Abdul Qadir is loved by his mother.
- As a small boy, he prefers to watch and wonder while the other children play.
- He always asks questions.

- He studies with teachers in the village, but his thirst for knowledge is unsatiated.
- He longs to attend university in Baghdad, but it is far away and too costly.
- His mother can see it's important. She takes on extra work and saves money.
- Eventually she arranges a camel caravansary for Abdul's safe passage to Baghdad.
- She sews forty gold coins into his coat.
- She reminds Abdul to "always be kind, and always be honest."
- As he rides on the camel's back, more questions come to Abdul's mind.
- Suddenly, the caravan is ambushed. The thieves take all they can find.
- They demand to know whether anyone has more. Abdul tells of the forty coins in his coat.
- The thieves are incredulous. One begins to take the coins.
- The other thief stops him. He asks Abdul why he admitted having the coins.
- Abdul tells of the promise of honesty he has made to his mother.
- The thieves are incredulous once more.
- They drop the stolen goods and leave.
- The caravansary continues its journey.
- Abdul studies. Eventually he becomes an imam and remains an inspiration to many.
- The thieves give up their dishonest ways.

Living with One Another

Ivarr's Tale

Recorded in Iceland in the 1200s, this story is said to be the first Western example of a psychotherapeutic approach to healing. King Eystein's sensitivity and deep listening skills continue to resonate as the most profound gift we can offer another person.

IN 1103, DURING THE REIGN of the "fair-haired kings" of Norway, King Magnus the Barefoot died. His three sons came to share the throne of Norway. How could this be?

King Olaf was never more than a figurehead; he died as a very young man.

King Sigurd sailed off, like a true Viking, to conquer distant lands.

King Eystein stayed in Norway to "tend the hearth." He built a new palace, an abbey, churches, halls, and trade centers. Most importantly, he built friendship with the people of Norway and beyond.

One man who enjoyed the king's friendship was the Icelandic bard Ivarr. The king loved Ivarr's music and merriment. He offered him a permanent position in his court and rewarded the bard well, with a fine apartment and plenty of gold.

Ivarr enjoyed the excellent conditions of his employment. He sent word to his brother, Thorstein, advising him to seek work in the King's court.

Thorstein was always ready to take advantage of a good opportunity. He immediately set sail from Iceland, filled with dreams of earning a great fortune.

But when he arrived, neither the king nor any of the court was much interested in Thorstein's skills as a fighter or a marksman. Instead, everywhere he went, he heard, "Ahh, you're Ivarr's brother. What a fine poet he is! Such a musician!"

Thorstein grew tired of living in the shadow of his brother and he decided to head back to Iceland. Ivarr was sad to see his brother go. As he waved goodbye, he begged Thorstein to go directly to Asta, Ivarr's one true love. "Tell her that I think of her day and night and that I'll be back in the summer to ask for her hand in marriage."

Thorstein nodded, and when he landed in Iceland, he kept his promise—at least so far as going directly to Asta's family farm. But instead of relaying Ivarr's message, he proposed to Asta.

What was Asta to think? A younger brother would surely have consulted with his older brother before proposing. This could only mean that Ivarr had found someone else. A little reluctantly, Asta agreed. The couple was soon married.

When word of the wedding spread to Norway, it was as though a black cloud descended over Ivarr. He could not sing. He could not play. There was not an ounce of merriment in him.

The King noticed, and he called Ivarr to his side.

"I can see that you are unhappy. Are you longing for adventure?"

"No," mumbled Ivarr.

"Do you wish for your own farm?"

"No."

"Are you homesick for Iceland?"

"No."

"Then it can only be a woman," reasoned the King. "But that is no problem. There is no woman who will refuse you once she sees my seal on your proposal."

"Not so," replied Ivarr.

"Well then," said the king, a little perplexed. "I do not wish to interfere with your affairs, but you must take your mind off this woman. Let me send you away on one of the ships heading south to Constantinople."

"I am no warrior."

"Let me buy you a farm."

"I am no farmer."

"Let me take you on a tour to all the grand homes of Norway and introduce you to all the most beautiful women."

"None will be as beautiful."

"Ahh," said the king. "Then all I can think to offer is very humble. It is nothing compared to all the riches you have just refused. But if you would like, you are welcome to come to me every evening when the affairs of the court are through. You can dine with me and tell me all about your one true love."

"I should like that very much," replied Ivarr.

And so it went. Every evening when the affairs of court were through, Ivarr went to sit with King Eystein and tell his story.

He told the king about Asta's beautiful blue eyes, her long flaxen braid, and her voice like a meadowlark. He told about her family and his own and their farms. One story at a time, Ivarr's dark cloud of sorrow lifted. One story at a time, the sun began to shine again for Ivarr. Finally, he was able to make merry once more.

It's hardly surprising that King Eystein came to be known as one of the great kings of Norway.

———————

FOR REFLECTION

- When have you felt like you were truly heard?
- What made it possible for you to be heard?
- When have you made an impact on another person's life by simply listening?

THEMES

acceptance, anger, brokenness, caring, compassion, covenant, depression, despair, empathy, friendship, generosity, grief, hope, hospitality, kindness, letting go, listening, love, patience, presence, relationships, sorrow, suffering, wealth, worth

PRINCIPLES

- Inherent worth and dignity of every person
- Justice, equity, and compassion in human relations
- Acceptance of one another and encouragement to spiritual growth

STORY MAP

- It's 1100 and Eystein is King of Norway. He is one of three brothers who share the throne.
- Ivarr works as the king's bard and is very successful.
- Ivarr encourages his brother to come to Norway.
- Ivarr's brother Thorstein is envious of the attention paid to Ivarr and returns home.
- Thorstein promises to bring a message to Ivarr's love.
- Thorstein betrays Ivarr and marries Ivarr's love.
- Ivarr's heart is broken.
- The King notices that Ivarr is unhappy and tries to guess what is wrong with his bard:
- Is he feeling underpaid?
- Is he craving adventure?
- Is he craving his own land?
- Ivarr responds "no" to all of these questions.
- The king reasons it can only be a woman who is making Ivarr unhappy.
- The king offers to help.
- Can the king force a divorce? No, it's impossible.
- Does Ivarr want to go overseas?

- Does Ivarr want a farm?
- Does Ivarr want to be introduced to other women?
- Ivarr responds "no" to all of these questions.
- The king offers to listen to Ivarr's story of lost love.
- Ivarr responds "yes" to this offer of kindness.
- Ivarr tells his story and slowly rediscovers a capacity for joy.
- It's not surprising that King Eystein was known as a great king, for he knew how to be a good listener.

The Meat
of the Tongue

It's refreshing when a poor man has the opportunity to teach his wealthy and powerful neighbor an important lesson. Set on the sultry coast of medieval East Africa, this Swahili story prompts a consideration of the most important kind of gift we can share with our loved ones.

LONG AGO, along the coast of East Africa, a sultan and sultana lived in the grandest of palaces.

The sultan spared no expense for his beloved sultana. She lived in the finest room and enjoyed every luxury she desired.

Each and every day, the sultan gave her new clothing or a new jewel and loved to look at her wearing it. Even after years of marriage, he was madly in love with the sultana.

But he was worried.

When they'd first met, she had sparkling eyes and bright red cheeks, broad hips and flesh that jiggled. But as the years had gone by, the sultana had grown pale and thin. Her eyes had become dull.

The sultan consulted his vizier, his doctor, every wise man he could find. None of their potions helped.

One advisor told him that beyond the palace walls, the wives of most of the poor fishermen had flesh that jiggled, and sparkle and color in their cheeks and eyes. In desperation, the sultan sent his advisors to uncover the fishermen's secrets.

The advisors wound their way into the humblest part of town, seeking an answer to the sultan's question. Most of the fishermen shrugged their shoulders.

Finally, down an especially narrow alleyway, the advisor found a man who cautiously mumbled, "It is the meat of the tongue."

When the sultan heard this, he was overjoyed by the simplicity of the cure!

He ordered his cooks to prepare the finest tongues they could buy. And so the sultana was served tongue of ox, tongue of gazelle, tongue of ostrich, tongue of tuna. Still she languished, remaining thin, pale, and nearly lifeless.

The sultan thought long and hard. Perhaps the fisherman who had revealed his secret could cure the sultana.

And so he sent word to ask whether the fisherman would consider caring for his beloved.

In exchange, the fisherman's plump wife could come and live at the palace.

The fisherman's wife was eager to experience a life of luxury.

The sultana was too weak to disagree.

The two women exchanged places.

Before long, the sultan heard that color had returned to the cheeks of his wife, that her eyes had begun to shine, and her hips were filling out.

73

Meanwhile in the palace, the poor fisherman's wife was growing thin, weak, and listless. More than anything, she wanted to go home.

How could this be? What was the poor fisherman's secret? [*You might ask your audience for their ideas.*]

The sultan personally accompanied the fisherman's wife home.
    There he was delighted to see the vibrancy of his own wife.

He told the fisherman how he'd been careful to feed first his wife and then the fisherman's wife "meat of the tongue," but it hadn't worked. He begged the fisherman to reveal more of his secret.
    The fisherman laughed and said, "Surely your vizier did not think I meant the meat of an animal's tongue? My wife flourishes because in the evening, we sit together, sharing nourishment in the form of jokes and songs and stories."

Turning to his wife, the sultan asked incredulously, "Is that why you thrive? Because of jokes and songs and stories?"

The sultana nodded, and at that moment the sultan resolved to change.

He did.
    When they returned together to the palace, they began a new regime. Each evening, when the sky was painted red and sun slanted in through the windows of the palace, the sultan and sultana sat together.

At first, talking together felt awkward.
    With practice, they became increasingly comfortable sharing stories of their lives. Now and then they joked or sang together.

All around them, the servants and advisors noticed that, even without new clothes or jewels, the sultana sparkled and smiled more than ever before. So too did the sultan.

FOR REFLECTION

- What are some ways that wealth or poverty can affect our relationships with others?
- What are some of the things that prevent us from spending enough time with the people we love? What helps?
- How does our quality of life change when we share stories?

THEMES

caring, class, compassion, connection, depression, dignity, failure, generosity, greed, happiness, hope, joy, kindness, listening, love, marriage, money, playfulness, presence, relationships, searching, simplicity, sorrow, wealth, worth

PRINCIPLES

- Acceptance of one another and encouragement to spiritual growth
- Free and responsible search for truth and meaning

STORY MAP

- There is a grand palace on the East African coast.
- The palace sits on a cliff. It is very ornate and beautifully furnished.
- People dress elegantly, especially the sultana.
- Each day, the sultan gives her new luxurious clothes or jewels. He loves to look at her wearing them.
- He is as madly in love with the sultana as ever, but he is worried.
- The sultana is languishing. Doctors and viziers know no cure.
- They hear a rumor that the poor fishermen's wives thrive.
- The advisors search for and finally find a fisherman who says the secret is "the meat of the tongue."
- The sultan orders cooks to prepare every kind of tongue meat, every day.
- The sultana continues to languish.

- The sultan asks a poor fisherman to care for the sultana and invites the fisherman's wife to live at the palace.
- All involved agree.
- The fisherman's wife is soon unhappy. Meanwhile, the sultana thrives.
- The two women return to their homes.
- The sultan vows to change his ways.
- At first, it is awkward for both the sultan and the sultana.
- Sharing stories, conversation, and song eventually grows easier. Both are far happier.

The Elephant
and the Dog

No matter how much luxury we enjoy, life is empty without the gift of friendship. Thank goodness it can arise between the most unlikely of characters! This story from India is perfect for celebrating friends and animals.

PERHAPS YOU'VE SEEN images of elephant families holding on to one another tail to trunk and trunk to tail, like true kin.

It isn't always so. The king had just one elephant. He lived alone in a magnificent stable with walls of inlaid marble, and bedding of the very finest hay.

If ever the elephant showed the least sign of an itch, his caregiver, the *mahout*, took him down to the river for a roll in the mud and a scrub in the water.

And when the elephant was hungry, he was served fine sweet rice with the freshest cabbages, bananas, oranges, and acacia leaves that were followed, always, by an elephant-sized sugar cube.

Really, that elephant had nothing to complain about, except boredom.

It was true. He spent much of his time rocking back and forth, forth and back, alone in his stable.

Meanwhile, a skinny, scrawny dog lived just outside the royal stable. He lurked alone in the shadows and rarely had enough to eat. But he did have one pleasure. When he saw the mahout arrive with the elephant's barrels full of food, he would sit just below the stable window to enjoy the sweet fragrances of rice, cabbages, bananas, and sugar. Sometimes it almost made his belly feel full.

One day, the stable door was left slightly ajar, just enough for the skinny, scrawny dog to squeeze through. He skulked in the shadows, quaking a little. What would the elephant do? Would he notice? [*You might shake your head, so the audience knows to say "no."*]

But the dog noticed. He noticed that when the elephant ate, he dropped all kinds of crumbs. The dog salivated. And when the elephant still seemed oblivious to him, the dog found courage. He crept right beneath that great big animal to feast on those crumbs.

Still, the elephant didn't seem to notice. Though, if you'd been looking carefully, you might have seen that he was rocking back and forth with more lilt and lightness.

The dog was too busy licking up the crumbs to see. When he finished eating, he retreated back into the shadows and fell asleep.

So it went. The dog crawled under the elephant to lick up the crumbs, and then retreated again. Did the elephant notice? [*You might shake your head so the audience knows to say "no."*] But the odd thing was that he spilled more crumbs with each passing day.

The dog grew healthier and livelier. And finally one day, the elephant looked down. The dog cowered a little. Was the elephant angry? [*You might shake your head, so the audience knows to say "no."*]

He was delighted. He reached out his trunk and wrapped it around the dog in a warm embrace. That night, the two slept cuddled together.

So it went. By night the two friends slept, cozy as could be. By day, they shared food and exchanged stories.

It was then that the mahout became conscious of the dog. Did he mind? [*You might shake your head again, so the audience knows to say "no."*] What did it matter if a dog wanted to lick up the crumbs?

Things might have continued in this happy way for a very long time, except that the mahout heard that a visiting merchant was looking for a dog. The mahout immediately thought of the stray dog in the stable. It didn't belong to anyone—surely it wouldn't matter if he sold it to earn a few extra coins for his family. Would it matter? [*Your audience will likely say "yes!"*] Did he do it anyway?

Sadly, he didn't seem to be aware that he shouldn't, and so he put the dog on a leash and brought it to the merchant. The merchant was delighted by the dog's shiny coat and healthy good looks. He paid a fine price and dragged the dog away.

The mahout continued to care for the elephant as usual, but it began to languish. The food was as plentiful as ever, the spa treatments were as frequent as ever, but the elephant had lost interest in everything. He lay listlessly on the stable floor.

Word spread. The king began to worry. What had happened to his elephant? Could the mahout explain? [*Cue your audience to say "no."*] When he couldn't say, the king called on his advisor for help.

At the stable, the advisor checked in the elephant's ears and throat. He checked his temperature and his pulse. The elephant wasn't sick. One look in the elephant's eyes told the advisor that the elephant was grieving.

Grieving? The King called for the mahout, who suddenly came to think of the dog that he'd sold. Of course! That was it! But he had no idea where the merchant lived.

The King issued a proclamation.

"Whoever has recently purchase a dog from the royal stable must return it at once." The news spread far and wide. Did it reach the ears of the merchant? [*Your audience will likely say "yes."*]

That dog had cried constantly since he'd been in the merchant's possession. The merchant was more than happy to release him. As soon as he did, the dog stopped whimpering and raced straight to the elephant's stable.

Was the elephant happy to see his good friend? [*Your audience will likely say "yes!"*]

Absolutely! He pulled himself up off the floor to wrap his trunk around the dog. They snuggled together for a very long time. Before long, the elephant's appetite returned.

Having a friend beside him was exactly the medicine he needed. It's some of the best medicine there is.

———

EXTENSION   You might want to relate the true story of Tarra and Bella, the elephant and dog who lived together at The Elephant Sanctuary in Tennessee. When Bella got sick, Tarra mourned.

FOR REFLECTION

- When and how does a friend move from being almost invisible to almost indispensable?
- What friendships between animals have you observed?
- When has a friend made a big difference in your life?
- What are some of the things that help create enduring friendship?

THEMES

caring, class, connection, depression, friendship, grief, happiness, hospitality, interdependence, joy, kindness, love, patience, poverty, privilege, relationships, wealth, worth

PRINCIPLES

- Inherent worth and dignity of every person
- World community with peace, liberty, and justice for all
- Respect for the interdependent web of all existence

- An elephant lives alone in a magnificent stable.
- It has excellent care from its mahout, with frequent baths, abundant food, a lovely stable, and thick bedding.
- The elephant enjoys all of this but finds life boring.
- A skinny dog lives outside the stable.
- The aroma of the elephant's food is its single pleasure.
- One day, the stable door is left open. The dog slinks inside.
- The elephant doesn't notice. The dog notices crumbs on the floor.
- The dog creeps beneath the elephant to eat. Still the elephant doesn't seem to notice.
- The dog sleeps in the shadows of the stable.
- The same pattern continues for several days. Only the dog is aware that the elephant drops more crumbs with each passing day.
- The dog grows healthier and livelier. Finally the elephant acknowledges him and is not angry.
- The elephant hugs the dog. The two sleep cuddled together.
- The two share food and stories and sleep side-by-side for several days.
- The mahout notices but doesn't mind.
- A visiting merchant arrives in the market looking for a dog.
- The mahout sells the dog.
- The elephant grows listless despite its usual good treatment.
- The king worries and calls on a special advisor who diagnoses that the elephant is grieving.
- The mahout recalls the dog but doesn't know where the merchant lives.
- The king issues a decree about returning the dog.
- The merchant hears it and is happy to return the dog. It has been crying incessantly.
- The dog and elephant are reunited. Having a friend is the best medicine.

Birds Learn about Friendship

Two birds illustrate the power of the platinum rule when they treat one another with respect and kindness; soon enough other birds want to follow suit. In this optimistic Burmese story, I've imagined the conversations between Crow and Pheasant.

THERE ARE 1,062 DIFFERENT KINDS of birds that make their homes in the jungles, wetlands, and along the coast of Burma. And once upon a time, those 1,062 kinds of birds did *not* get along. They were always making a terrible ruckus.

"Why do you flap your wings so fast?"

"Your feathers are too red."

"With that technique, you'll never be able to catch a worm."

Often the birds got so carried away that they said, "I'm a better bird than you." The reply was always, "No, I'm a better bird than you." There was no friendship amongst the birds. And not much fun either.

Finally, Pheasant grew weary. He didn't want to quarrel, so when Crow came along, ready to pick an argument, Pheasant said, "Crow, you're a better bird than me."

Crow was surprised! Those words warmed his heart and he replied politely, "No, Pheasant, you are a better bird than me."

Pheasant's heart felt warm. The two struck up a conversation. They got to know one another and found that they got along very well. Before long, they decided to live side-by-side. The two birds enjoyed one another very much. Now their conversations were completely different than they had been in the days of argument.

One day when Pheasant stood stock-still, Crow noticed and said, "That was a good way to avoid being seen by enemies." Another time when Crow was building a nest, Pheasant said, "Those sticks will make a good strong nest. But have you thought about a way to make it a little softer inside?" Crow looked at the nest and then at his chest. He began to add some downy feathers.

Talking and getting along like that made it easy to learn from each other and be together. The two friends' affection for one another was obvious. The other birds were surprised. How could Pheasant and Crow spend so much time together without quarreling? Some decided to test the friendship.

"Pheasant, why do you spend so much time with that good-for-nothing Crow?"

"You mustn't say that!" replied Pheasant. "Crow is a better bird than I and he honors me by living with me."

The next day, they went to Crow.

"Crow, why do you spend so much time with that good-for-nothing Pheasant?"

You mustn't say that!" replied Crow. "Pheasant is a better bird than I and he honors me by living with me."

The birds were deeply impressed by Crow and Pheasant's attitude to one another. They began to wonder, "Why do we always fight and quarrel?" They watched how Crow and Pheasant treated one another and soon learned that it wasn't so difficult to be kind. They also learned that when they practiced compassion in the manner of Crow and Pheasant, life was far more enjoyable.

That is how friendship and respect developed among the birds.

VARIATIONS   You can help your audience relate to the story by inserting asides into it. For example, you might add, "Have you ever heard people talking like that?" at several points in the tale. Or toward the end, you might add, "Have you ever noticed that it's easier to listen and learn when someone is kind?"

FOR REFLECTION

- When have you noticed people behaving like the birds at the beginning of the story?
- What can help change a person's behavior, especially when they are not being kind to one another?
- When have you noticed that one person's positive behavior influences the way others behave?
- How does criticism help or hinder your learning? When has kindness helped you learn something?

THEMES

acceptance, anger, caring, change, choice, community, compromise, conflict, connection, culture, diversity, friendship, gratitude, growth, happiness, kindness, letting go, limitations, listening, love, loyalty, multiculturalism, peace, reconciliation, relationships, respect, teamwork, trust

PRINCIPLES

- Inherent worth and dignity of every person
- Acceptance of one another and encouragement to spiritual growth
- World community with peace, liberty, and justice for all

STORY MAP

- There are many kinds of birds in Burma.
- None of the birds are friends with other types of birds.
- Criticism and cruelty are widespread among the birds.
- Pheasant doesn't like the fighting and surprises Crow with kindness.
- Crow reciprocates and treats Pheasant kindly.
- The birds continue their kindness toward one another.
- Crow and Pheasant become neighbors.
- The other birds are suspicious of this friendship and try to test Crow and Pheasant's loyalty to one another.
- Both Crow and Pheasant remain true to one another.
- The other birds are inspired and change their ways.
- The bird kingdom is a friendlier and happier place.

Polite Peculiarities

Grace comes in many guises. In this playful story from China, quick thinking rescues an awkward social situation and we see that creativity can be an important tool for maintaining a healthy relationship.

IN THE GUANGDONG PROVINCE of southern China, a mother was very excited. She was going to visit her married daughter. It was a long journey, and when she arrived, only the daughter and her mother-in-law were at home. And so the three women were alone together for the evening meal.

Just when the food was about to be served, the lights in the room suddenly went out. The mother-in-law murmured, "I'll rekindle the lamps."

Hearing her leave the room and thinking she was alone with her daughter, the mother took the opportunity to offer advice: "You remember, don't you, that it is our custom here in Guangdong to always offer the choicest food to our guests. The best way to do so is to turn the side of the platter that holds the most succulent meats, the crispest vegetables, the ripest fruit, and the thickest pastries toward the guest."

When her daughter didn't reply, she emphasized her fatigue with a sigh. Then she continued, "Of course, it is especially important to follow this custom when serving a relative who is visiting from afar."

Just then, the lights came back on.

To her horror, the mother realized that she had not been talking to her daughter. Her daughter had gone to sort out the lamps and she had been talking to her daughter's mother-in-law!

There was a momentary awkward silence.

Finally, she smiled. "I must tell you, my esteemed new relation, that I have a strange affliction. If ever I am visiting and the lights suddenly go out, I begin to say absolutely nonsensical things. Not a word I say is in my control; nor should it be believed. It is only when the lights come back on that I return to my senses."

After a few moments, the mother-in-law smiled and replied, "I understand completely. I have a similarly strange affliction. If ever I am visiting—even in my own home—and the lights suddenly go out, I become stone-deaf and do not hear a word that is said until the lights come back on."

The daughter had no idea what was going on, but she smiled at the two older women and felt certain that the evening would go well.

Indeed, it did.

FOR REFLECTION

- When does not listening serve us well?
- What are some of your tools for rescuing an awkward situation?
- In what other ways might the mothers have rescued their situation?

THEMES

acceptance, anger, blame, caring, compassion, connection, creativity, dignity, empathy, family, forgiveness, generosity, hospitality, humility, imagination, kindness, letting go, playfulness, relationships

PRINCIPLES

- Justice, equity, and compassion in human relations
- Acceptance of one another and encouragement to spiritual growth

- A mother is excited about visiting her daughter far away at her new home with her husband's family.
- Only the daughter and her mother-in-law are at home when the mother visits.
- At dinner, the lamp goes out.
- One of the women says she'll fetch a new light.
- In the dark, the mother reminds her daughter of social etiquette and the importance of giving the best food to the guest.
- The lights come back on and the mother is horrified. She was speaking to the mother-in-law!
- The mother tells her daughter's mother-in-law that she has a strange affliction. She speaks nonsense when the lights goes out.
- The mother-in-law reveals her own strange ailment. She cannot hear anything when the lights go out.
- The daughter is perplexed by the strange statements, but certain all will go well.

The Sign
of the Tassel

Living in relationship is an ongoing process of learning. While stressing that change is possible, this Middle Eastern story offers a humorous solution for dealing with a surly person. When we take another person's feelings into consideration, our own behavior often improves.

DOWN THE STREET and around seven corners, a woman and man were married.

They loved one another. But very soon after the marriage, the woman was sorry to discover that her husband often came home in a foul mood. One thing or another happened during the day that made him grumpy or angry. He carried this burden home with him and was not at all shy about sharing it with her.

"This cannot go on," thought the woman. She contemplated what to do until finally one day she said, "Husband of mine, I know that your work is difficult and causes you grief some days. And I've noticed that on those days you come home angry."

Her husband nodded, and she continued, "Husband, I think things will go better if you could warn me before you get home on the days when you are angry. Then I can take your bad humor into consideration and treat you carefully."

He liked the idea, thought for a moment, and then said, "I wear my red fez every day."

Who wouldn't, it was very elegant!

"I could flip the long black tassel that hangs to the side over to the front of my fez. Then you'd know and could take my bad humor into account."

"Yes, why not?" said the wife with enthusiasm and added, with a little hesitation, "The only thing is that I am sometimes angry too."

He nodded as she continued, "So I think it would only be fair to you if I also warned you with a sign when I am angry. I have a lovely white apron that I rarely use. Perhaps I should wear it on the days when I am in a foul humor."

"Why not?" said the husband, "then I can take your anger into consideration too."

And so they adopted the plan.

The very next day, everything seemed to go wrong for the husband and, as he walked home, his anger grew with each step. By the time he rounded the corner on to their street, he was furious. But when he reached their house, he remembered the plan and what did do? [*You might pause here, and after the other questions that follow, to allow your audience to reply.*] He quickly flipped the tassel around to the front side of his elegant red fez.

The woman had been anticipating her husband's arrival and was looking out the window. When she saw the tassel, what did she do? She quickly ran to put her apron on!

The husband opened the door, and when he saw the white apron, he thought, "Oh dear, it will never do for us both to be angry. We might come to blows." And so he quickly flipped the tassel back around to the side of his elegant red fez. He did his very best to be pleasant and to treat her with kindness and compassion. She also managed to be kind.

They had a lovely evening.

A few days later, the same thing happened. He was angry but caught himself in time before he got home and what did he do? Of course, he flipped the tassel around. And the woman? As soon as she saw his fez, she put her apron on. When he saw her apron, he rearranged his tassel and they managed to be perfectly pleasant with one another again.

The same scenario, with the tassel and then the apron and then the tassel, happened over and again, several more times.

Finally the husband said, "It is very strange. Every time I come home angry, you are angry too."

"It is strange indeed," replied the woman, "But it is good that we are able to put our anger aside." And then she added, "We human beings have been cursed with tempers, but we are also blessed with wisdom. Perhaps we could both agree to end our bad habit of being angry, and decide instead to always be kind and compassionate to one another."

"That would be wise," said the man.

And that is what they did.

FOR REFLECTION

- What are some other ways that the woman might have tackled the problem? What are some of the differences between the solution presented in the story and tools like non-violent or compassionate communication?
- When has a non-verbal cue caused you to change your behavior?
- How might making an agreement similar to this help in one of the important relationships in your life?
- What would help an agreement like this be a stepping stone to long-term change?

THEMES

acceptance, anger, assumptions, caring, change, choice, commitment, compassion, compromise, conflict, covenant, empathy, forgiveness, happiness, honesty, kindness, letting go, listening, love, marriage, patience, peace, presence, relationships, responsibility, self-care, self-respect, teamwork

PRINCIPLES

- Justice, equity, and compassion in human relations
- Acceptance of one another and encouragement to spiritual growth

STORY MAP

- A man and woman marry.
- The woman soon learns that her husband is often grumpy in the evening.
- She thinks about the best way to deal with his bad temper.
- The wife suggests that they warn one another when they are in a bad mood.
- The husband agrees to move the tassel on his red fez forward when he comes home in a bad mood.
- The wife admits to an occasional bad temper. She says she'll wear a certain apron on those days.
- The next day, the husband has a bad day and is increasingly grumpy as he walks home. He remembers to flip the tassel on his fez to the front to indicate his bad mood.
- The wife sees this sign out the window and puts on her apron to show she is also in a bad mood.
- When the husband sees his wife's apron, he decides to curb his bad temper and be kind.
- The same pattern continues for a few days.
- The husband notices and says it's strange that she is in a bad mood whenever he is.
- She agrees but comments that they have learned it's possible to put grumpiness aside.
- The couple agrees to always put their grumpiness aside and treat one another with kindness instead.

Kassa, the Strong One

Pride leaves us vulnerable to a fall, especially when we forget that a curious and creative mind can be far more powerful than brute strength. I love the surprise twist in this story from the Mende people of West Africa.

Kassa Kenna Genanina was very strong. And he knew it.

One day he went hunting. His friends Iri ba Jelemi and Congo ba Farra came with him. They had rifles, but did Kassa? No! He carried only a long iron pole.

Guess who took down twenty antelope? Was it Iri or Congo? No! It was Kassa Kenna Genanina, with his long iron pole.

Iri and Congo helped Kassa drag the antelope into a clearing. Now they needed firewood. Kassa said to Iri, "You guard the meat, while Congo and I go and get some firewood."

So Iri stayed in the clearing. Before long a huge bird swooped overhead. It called out, "Shall I take some meat, or shall I take you?"

What would you say? "Take the meat! Take the meat!" [*Encourage your audience to call out the answer with you.*] That is what I would say, and that is what Iri said.

After a time, Kassa Kenna Genanina and Congo ba Farra returned to the clearing. Kassa saw immediately that one antelope was missing and said, "What happened? Where is the meat?" When Iri told him about the bird, Kassa shouted, "You should have told the bird to take you!"

Iri sighed, and Kassa turned to Congo, "This time Iri will come with me to gather more firewood. You can guard the meat." So Congo stayed in the clearing. Before long, a huge bird swooped overhead. It called out, "Shall I take some meat, or shall I take you?"

What would you say? "Take the meat! Take the meat!" [*Encourage your audience to say it with you.*] That is what I would say, and that is what Congo said.

After a time, Kassa and Iri returned to the clearing. Kassa saw immediately that one antelope was missing and said, "What happened? Where is the meat?" When Congo told him about the bird, Kassa shouted, "You should have told the bird to take you! This time you two go and get firewood, and I will guard the meat."

Before long, a huge bird swooped overhead. It called out, "Shall I take some meat, or shall I take you?"

"Neither!" shouted Kassa Kenna Genanina as he jumped up and swung his long pole. He swung it again and again until he had knocked that bird right out of sight. He puffed up his chest with pride, but he was too quick.

A feather had come loose from that bird. It drifted down, down, down, and landed on Kassa Kenna Genanina's chest. Ooh! It was heavy. It knocked him right to the ground. Struggle as he might, he couldn't get up again!

After a time—what felt like an impossibly long time to Kassa—his two friends returned to the clearing. They tried and tried to lift that feather. But it was heavy! They could not budge the feather, and so Kassa remained trapped on the ground.

A young woman had entered the clearing by then. She carried her baby on her back. She was surprised to see strong Kassa stuck lying on the ground. She was surprised that his friends couldn't help him.

But do you think she knew about the way Kassa liked to brag?

Do you think she knew that Kassa was sometimes unkind?

Do you think she saw the world a little differently than Kassa saw it?

Oh yes!

Do you think that young woman was curious?

Oh yes!

Her curiosity gave her the courage to walk right over to Kassa Kenna Genanina. She saw that feather and was still more curious. She didn't try to pick it up. Instead, she bent right over Kassa, took a deep breath, and blew as hard as she could. The feather lifted up and up. The woman caught it in her hand, gave it to her baby to play with, and walked out of the clearing.

Congo and Iri smiled a little.

Kassa Kenna Genanina stared after her for a very long time.

I wonder whether he treated his friends a little differently after that.

I wonder whether his friends treated him a little differently.

I wonder what that woman and her baby did with the feather. Perhaps they've used it to tickle away someone else's foolish pride.

FOR REFLECTION

- What might the feather that weighs down the great hero represent?
- When have you been weighed down by a feather? How did you come out from under that weight?
- When have "fresh eyes" helped solve a problem for you?

THEMES

arrogance, character, courage, doubt, failure, fear, humility, imagination, leadership, limitations, playfulness, power, pride, strength, weakness

PRINCIPLES

- Inherent worth and dignity of every person
- Free and responsible search for truth and meaning

STORY MAP

- Kassa is strong (and conceited).
- He goes hunting with his friends Iri and Congo.
- They have guns, but Kassa has only a long pole.
- Who takes down twenty antelope? Kassa!
- Iri guards the antelope stash while the others search for firewood.
- A huge bird threatens Iri. Iri gives the bird an antelope.
- Kassa returns and is outraged by this.
- Congo now guards the antelope stash while the others search for firewood.
- A huge bird threatens Congo. Congo gives the bird an antelope.
- Kassa returns and is outraged by this.
- Kassa guards the antelope stash while the others search for firewood.
- The huge bird threatens Kassa. Kassa swings his pole at the bird.
- He scares the bird off but a feather falls and lands on Kassa.
- The feather knocks him down.
- Kassa tries to move the feather off his chest, but it is impossible!
- Congo and Iri both try. It is impossible for them.
- A woman enters the clearing carrying a baby on her back.
- She sees Kassa and the feather. She bends down and blows the feather off Kassa's chest.
- She catches the feather and gives it to her baby as a toy.
- Will Kassa treat others differently now?
- Will the woman use the feather to tease away another man's foolish pride?

▽◦△◦▽

Practicing
Generosity

△◦▽◦△

The Magic Spring

In this Korean folktale, greed and generosity each have their own reward, and spending time in nature is more restorative than we might imagine. The unpredictable way the characters' wish comes true is a reminder that following our calling has great power.

LONG AGO in the Korean countryside, there were a husband and wife who had lived a long life together. Their home was small, and they had little in the way of wealth, but they were mostly happy.

Their only sorrow was that, although they had hoped and prayed for a child for many years, they had never been blessed with one. In their old age, they comforted themselves with the love they had for one another.

The couple were friendly with the single man who lived on the farm next door. They helped one another with some of the bigger jobs on their two farms.

Over the years, the couple couldn't help but notice that their neighbor was a little greedy. He always wanted the best tools and always took the biggest share when they harvested together. They shrugged off his greediness, hopeful that he would change one day.

The couple loved their small farm, especially because it was nestled next to a beautiful forest. In springtime, they enjoyed searching for wildflowers and loved to hear the birds sing.

One spring day, while the husband was sowing seeds in their field, he noticed an especially beautiful birdsong. The notes were crisp and clear; he felt as though it were calling to him, "Come here, come here!" He couldn't resist the sound of the bird. He set down his tools and followed it into the forest. Each time he came close, the bird flew off again. He followed it, further and deeper into the forest.

Finally, the bird stopped. The man saw it alight. The branch where it rested arched over a beautiful little spring that bubbled and gurgled in rhythm with the bird's song. He sat down to enjoy the private symphony.

When his ears and heart were full, he prepared to return home. He was thirsty though, so he leaned over the stream to enjoy a good long drink of the fresh spring water. How refreshing it was.

He bowed in thanks to the bird, stood up, and began to walk home. The water had been even more refreshing than he first thought. His legs felt longer and stronger, and there was a real bounce to his step.

When he arrived home, his wife looked at him oddly. "What is it?" he asked in a voice that was unusually clear.

His wife answered slowly, "The frog in your throat is gone, you are taller, you look stronger, and your wrinkles have disappeared!"

The husband felt his arms. They were as muscular as they had been many years ago. "It must be the spring," he whispered. And with awe in his voice, he told his wife about following the bird. She responded slowly, "You are young again! The bird led you to the fountain of youth!"

The next morning, they agreed that life would be best for them both if the wife also drank from the spring.

They made their way into the forest and what did they hear?

They followed the sound of the bird all the way to the spring. They enjoyed the symphony, the woman drank her fill of the water, and as she walked home, her step was light and sprightly. She had become a young woman once more.

Not many days had passed before a neighbor came by. When he saw the young couple, he demanded, "Who are you? Where are my neighbors? You look exactly like they looked forty years ago!"

When he realized that they were indeed his neighbors, he demanded to know their secret.

They'd barely begun to tell him about the spring. . .

[*You might ask your audience what they suppose he did.*]

He hurried off into the forest.

He didn't come back that evening, and the next day when he still hadn't returned, the couple began to worry. They made their way back to the spring.

[*You might ask your audience what they heard.*]

Instead of bird song, they heard a baby crying. It was a little boy—none other than their neighbor.

"He drank too much," said the husband.

"We can't leave him here," said the wife.

She bent down, picked up the baby, and carried him home.

He was the baby they had hoped and prayed for, and they raised him with love.

Some say that the boy grew up to be a generous soul.

———

FOR REFLECTION

- When have you felt called to do something? How have you recognized that calling? How did following the calling affect you?
- Having "too much of a good thing" is always a possibility. How do we know when to stop?

THEMES

aging, awe, beauty, calling, change, choice, discernment, environment, ethics, generosity, greed, happiness, limitations, love, marriage, nature, relationships, self-care, spirituality, transformation, youth

PRINCIPLES

- Acceptance of one another and encouragement to spiritual growth
- Free and responsible search for truth and meaning

STORY MAP

- A husband and wife live in the Korean countryside.
- They are happy with each other but sad not to have a child.
- They have friendly relations with a neighbor though they notice he is greedy.
- The couple loves their farm location next to a forest with wildflowers and birdsong.
- One day, the husband is in the field and hears a beautiful birdsong.
- He feels like the bird is calling him and follows the sound.
- He follows it deep into the forest, where he finally sees the beautiful bird sitting over a spring.
- He enjoys the music, gets thirsty, and drinks from the spring.
- He feels refreshed, thanks the bird, and returns home.
- His wife barely recognizes the youthful man.
- They realize he has drunk from the fountain of youth.
- The next morning they agree it's best for both if the woman does the same.
- They follow the bird to the spring. They listen and enjoy the bird's song, and the woman drinks the water.
- The wife is now young. They return home.
- The neighbor comes by and barely recognizes his youthful neighbors.
- He demands an explanation and then hurries to the forest to find the spring.
- He hasn't returned by the next day and the couple worries.
- They go to the spring and realize their neighbor drank too much when they find a baby there.
- They recognize that their wish for a baby has come true and bring home the baby to raise it.
- Some say the boy grows up to be generous.

A Gift for Grandfather

"If not now, when? If not me, who?" Community, partici-pation, and sharing are central ideas in this folktale from the Bamum people of Cameroon. It is retold here in the modern context of a birthday party. I've taken the liberty of picturing the characters learning their lesson and added the following year's party to the story. In most versions of the story, the gift is wine. The idea to use honey is from story-teller Bill Gordh.

GRANDFATHER'S BIRTHDAY WAS COMING. Family and friends would gather. But what to bring him? What gift would be right?

A nice sweater? Socks? A new shirt? No! He hadn't even opened the packages from last year. A book, a painting? No! His shelves and walls were crowded already. What to do?

Most of all, Grandfather liked to be at home, sitting in his chair, drinking tea with honey.

Honey! That was it. Grandfather had a beautiful big crock jar that sat empty on his shelf. They would fill it with enough honey to last the year. Word spread from one family member to another, and from one friend to the other. Soon everyone knew that they were each to bring a jar of honey to pour into grandfather's big crock. It would be a communal gift.

Jane was going to the party. She didn't have any honey, and she didn't have much money. What to do? She thought and thought some more. And then an idea came to her.

It's safe to say it wasn't the best idea, but Jane really wanted to go and she really wanted to be part of the gift. So she poured some water into a small jar and added a pinch of food coloring so that it was golden in color and looked just like honey.

She told herself, "No one will notice once I add it to the big jar. Besides that, it will make the honey easier to pour."

The day of the party came. The guests arrived, and one guest after another poured their small jars of honey into Grandfather's big crock. Jane poured hers in too. Before long, the crock was filled to the brim with honey, and it was time to present it to Grandfather.

"What's this?" he asked.

A few guests offered clues.

Some made buzzing sounds, others licked their lips.

[*You might invite audience participation
by putting your hand to your ear.*]

"Could it be honey?" said Grandfather, "How wonderful!" He dipped in a spoon to sample the golden liquid and lifted it to his lips. He smacked a few times, looking a little puzzled.

"It has a fine golden color," he said hesitantly, "But it tastes like water."

Jane's cheeks burned a bright red.

John's cheeks were equally rosy. Gillian covered her eyes and Jim covered his mouth. Jason looked down.

They had all played the same trick as Jane!

None of them thought it would make much of a difference if they brought water instead of honey, but now each and every one of them was embarrassed. It was an awkward moment.

Luckily, Grandfather laughed and said, "I have another birthday coming next year!"

You can bet that the next year, when Grandfather's birthday came again, everyone was sure to bring the very best honey possible. They poured their small jars into Grandfather's crock, and when he tasted it, "Mmmm!"

[*You might invite audience participation
by putting your hand to your ear.*]

Grandfather said that he could taste the flavor of each person's gift. There was a hint of orange blossom from Jane's honey, and fireweed from John's. There were the scents of clover, buckwheat, and wildflowers from Jim, Gillian, and Jason's contributions.

Grandfather smacked his lips. "This is the most delicious honey ever!"

The party was a much happier one!

FOR REFLECTION

- What are some of the best gifts we can give others?
- When does it feel difficult to bring real "honey" (be your most generous/kind/honest self)?
- What inspires you to offer your best in a community endeavor?

THEMES

blame, choice, community, conscience, covenant, ethics, failure, generosity, greed, guilt, honesty, integrity, interdependence, regret, responsibility, shame, teamwork, trust, truth, unity

PRINCIPLES

- Justice, equity, and compassion in human relations
- Right of conscience and use of the democratic process
- World community with peace, liberty, and justice for all

- Jane's grandfather's birthday is coming up.
- It's difficult to choose a gift. Should she buy him books or a sweater? No.
- But he likes tea with honey. Should she buy him honey? Yes.
- Word spreads around Jane's family. Everyone will bring some to fill her grandfather's big empty honey crock.
- Jane has no money and so decides to bring colored water to the party.
- On the day of the party, everyone brings honey and pours it into the crock.
- Jane's grandfather sees the gift and asks what it is. The guests offer clues.
- Grandfather tries the honey and looks surprised. The honey tastes like water.
- Jane and the rest of the family are embarrassed. They all brought colored water.
- Grandfather reminds them he has another birthday coming up next year.
- Next year, everyone brings good honey, of all varieties and flavors.
- Grandfather says he can taste all of the individual contributions.

Ukko's Bread

This moral tale from Finland uses humor to poke at the challenge of being generous and the human tendency to find ways to justify our less honorable behavior. The traditional cautionary ending is harsh. I have offered hope in an alternate ending by depicting what might have happened had the woman decided to change her stingy ways.

LONG AGO IN FINLAND, people told stories about the great god Ukko. Sometimes when he visited the birch forests of Finland, he took human form.

One day he came upon a small cottage. Through the window, he could see a woman with her arms up to her elbows in bread dough. He immediately thought of the delicious taste of freshly baked bread. It made him hungry.

He knocked at the door. The woman couldn't open it, of course, with her hands all doughy, but she called out, "Come in! Hurry up; don't let the cold air in!"

Ukko bent his head as he stepped inside. The woman had no idea who he was. She took him for a traveler or a beggar—and carried on with her work.

Ukko tried to be friendly. But as he chatted about the wind and the weather, he didn't take his eyes off the bread dough. The woman grew a little irritated and finally said, "The bread isn't baked yet."

"Ahhh," said Ukko. "Don't worry. A hungry man doesn't mind waiting." The woman wanted him out of her house. She said, "You're more than welcome. But for now, take a walk in the woods. Come back at nightfall and I'll give you some." Off Ukko went, full of expectation.

The woman soon finished kneading her dough. She stretched and folded and tucked in the edges to form a beautiful and very large loaf of bread.

[You might make these motions with your hands and invite your listeners to do the same. Repeat again each time the woman reshapes the loaf.]

She was about to set it out to rise, but then she thought, "It's too big. My visitor can't be *that* hungry."

She took her knife, cut that loaf in half, then stretched and folded and tucked in the edges to form a beautiful medium-sized loaf of bread.

She stepped back to admire it and thought, "It is still too big. He can't be *that* hungry."

The woman continued forming loaves over and again by stretching and folding and tucking . . . and then deciding that they were too big.

Finally when she had formed a loaf that was barely as large as her fist, she was satisfied. She knew that it would taste delicious. She let it rise first and then baked it.

There was a knock at the door. It was Ukko, of course.

"Come in! Hurry up; don't let the cold air in!" called the woman.

She quickly presented "the beggar" with the bun she had prepared for him.

Traditional Ending

Ukko gasped in surprise at the small size of the loaf. He saw the other loaves cooling on her table top even as she tried to encourage him out the door.

Ukko stood stock still. His shock had turned to outrage. With a blink, he turned that woman into a woodpecker! As she shrunk in size, he shouted, "Stingy you were, and hungry you'll be!"

Imagine that, the woman a woodpecker! What a change! Her beautiful red scarf became the bright feathers on her head; her dark dress became her black back and long wings. She looked down at them and could not recognize herself. She flapped those wings and found she could fly!

She flew right out of her house. At first it was thrilling, to move so swiftly through the air. But before long, she was tired and hungry. Flying took energy! And food was hard to come by. She had to keep flying to find it.

She flew here and she flew there. No matter how many trees she pecked at, no matter how much sap she slurped, she was always hungry. How many of you have heard a woodpecker pecking? The tap-tapping is proof that she is searching to this day.

What a difference being generous would have made! Perhaps she'd be baking bread still and we might all have had some!

Alternate Ending

[*If you choose to use the Matryoshka doll as described below (a traditional Russian doll that is actually a series of nesting dolls, with each containing a smaller version), show it to your listeners at the beginning of the story when the woman is first introduced. You might say something like "Through the window, he could see a woman who looked a little like this Matryoshka doll. She had her arms up to her elbows in bread. . . ."*]

He couldn't help but gasp a little in surprise at the small size. He thanked her politely before carrying on his way.

The woman watched him go. She had seen the disappointment on his face. She felt herself shrinking smaller and smaller.

[*Take apart the Matryoshka doll to show each smaller
one nesting inside. Continue until you're able to
show the smallest doll.*]

Smaller and smaller. Until finally she was just a very little, tiny person. A little, tiny, and very sad person. She wished she had been better at sharing.

As soon as she began wishing to be better at sharing, she noticed some warmth in her chest, all around her heart. It reminded her that she could be a big-hearted person. She could be generous.

She reached for some dough, as much dough as her tiny self could manage, and she began to knead it, stretch it, and fold it into a loaf of bread. It was a small loaf, but it was the best she could do. "I will give this to Ukko!" she thought.

And as soon as she had that thought, she felt her heart grow warm and herself grow bigger.

[*Close second smallest doll around smallest doll.*]

She reached for more dough, as much dough as her little self could manage. She added it to the other dough. She began to knead it, stretch it, and fold it into a loaf of bread. It was a small loaf, but it was the *best* she could do. "I will give this to Ukko!" she thought.

She did this over and again until, finally, the woman was her usual size.

[*Continue closing one doll around another until the
largest doll contains all the others.*]

She reached for more dough—not quite all of it—for her family needed some bread too. But she took as much as she could, added it to the dough, and then began to knead it, stretch it, and fold it into a lovely loaf of bread. It was the best she could do. "I will give this to Ukko!" she thought as she put the loaf in the oven.

Guess what?

There was a knock at her door.

Ukko came back.

She gave him the bread, and Ukko was very grateful. The bread was delicious. And the woman was grateful too, that she'd found a way to be generous and still feed her family.

FOR REFLECTION

- When have you struggled to be generous? What makes it difficult?
- When have you regretted your behavior? What do you do to overcome regret?

THEMES

caring, character, choice, compassion, conscience, failure, generosity, greed, guilt, kindness, letting go, redemption, regret, sacrifice, self-respect, service, shame, transcendence, transformation, work, worry

PRINCIPLES

- Inherent worth and dignity of every person
- Justice, equity, and compassion in human relations
- Acceptance of one another and encouragement to spiritual growth
- World community with peace, liberty, and justice for all

NOTE   Nesting dolls and boxes are known from as early as 1000 CE in both China and Japan. The Matryoshka figure of the famous Russian nesting doll is believed to symbolize motherhood. The first one of its type was carved in the late nineteenth century. The dolls have also been carved in a wide variety of shapes as animals, fairy tale characters, and political leaders. The tradition of carving the dolls as fairy tale characters sets precedence for using them to illustrate a story. Of course this story is Finnish, and so my use of the doll crosses cultural lines. You might also use nesting boxes or bowls.

- In Finland, the great god Ukko takes human form.
- Ukko comes to a small cottage and encounters a woman making bread.
- The woman thinks Ukko is a beggar and is impatient with him.
- She finally tells Ukko to come back later, when the bread is baked.
- She begins shaping a loaf for Ukko, decides it's too large, removes some dough, and reshapes the now smaller loaf.
- She repeats the shrinking process several times until the bread is the size of her fist.

Traditional Ending

- Ukko returns and is outraged.
- He turns the woman into a woodpecker.
- At first the woman enjoys flying, but then she gets hungry.
- She can never satisfy her hunger. She spends her days forever pecking (and reminding us not to be greedy).

Alternate Ending

- Ukko returns and is disappointed.
- In her feeling of shame, the woman begins to shrink.
- The woman wishes she'd been more generous and, with the wish, senses her warm heart.
- As her smallest self, she makes the largest loaf possible.
- She grows in size, then reshapes the loaf even larger. This causes her to grow again.
- This is repeated several times until she is back to her normal size.
- She now forms a loaf that is just right for Ukko.
- Ukko returns and is grateful. So is the woman.

Primroses
for Gold

According to the fairy folk in this old English story, some-one natural in their way of being is beautiful. In it, a young girl's authenticity and purity are rewarded with a gift, while a greedy and conniving miser receives a very different kind of reward.

IT WAS LONG AGO, in Somerset, in the southwest of England. It was springtime, and the forest was full of flowers.

A whole parcel of children was there. They'd had a picnic, and now they leapt and cavorted among the yellow blossoms that were everywhere. The primroses were so abundant on the forest floor that you could hardly see that the children had been busy picking bouquets. But when you looked at the children, you saw posies, nosegays, sprays, and corsages clutched in their hands and tucked into their buttonholes.

One little girl was especially enchanted by the beautiful flow-ers. She was having such a marvelous time picking them that she didn't notice how far from the others she was wandering.

She was the youngest of them all and as good as gold. She had no idea that she was heading down toward Goblin Combe, all on her own. Suddenly she was there! Oh dear! Her mum had said she should never go there. Not alone.

Tears began to well up in her eyes. They spilled over and down onto her dress like summer rain. She threw herself against a rock, sighing and sobbing and apologizing.

The fairy folk who lived inside that rock heard her. They opened up the door to the rock, and when they peaked out, they could see she was a dear little soul. They spilled out of that rock and comforted the girl.

"There, there," they tutted and whispered as they patted her on the back. They had a ball of pure gold and they gave it to her. They said it was all on account of the primroses she was carrying and of her being as good as gold. [*You might say, "good as _____" and allow your audience to fill in the blank, here and later when the line is repeated.*] Then they led her safely home.

Before long, the entire village was abuzz.

"Imagine that! A golden ball! All on account of a posy of primroses!" Her story spread like dandelion seeds in the wind.

There was a miser in the village. He spent his days counting piles of gold and conniving how to add more gold to his piles. He was often heard saying, "there's nothing as good as gold!"

When he heard about the small girl's bounty, the money lender was envious! He too wanted a golden ball. No. No. Wait a minute. He wanted every single golden ball that the fairies had.

He came up with what he thought was a good idea and headed to the forest to pick primroses. He gathered posies, nosegays, sprays, and corsages. He picked until his arms and his pockets overflowed with flowers. When he was finished, there weren't many primroses left to brighten the forest floor.

The miser hurried to Goblin Combe with his huge cache of flowers and pounded on the fairy rock. When he saw it open, he rushed inside.

It turned out that it wasn't the right day, nor the right number of primroses, and he wasn't a dear little soul nor was he as good as gold.

So the fairies took him, and that miserly man was never seen again.

Oh dear.

FOR REFLECTION

- When have you been so enraptured by the beauty of nature that you've lost track of all time?
- What might the golden ball represent? What rewards come out of authenticity and purity?
- When are we like the money lender? Who might he represent today?

THEMES

arrogance, authenticity, character, children, Earth, environment, ethics, greed, integrity, kindness, nature, stewardship, wealth

PRINCIPLE

- Respect for the interdependent web of all existence

STORY MAP

- In Somerset, in spring, the forest is full of golden primroses.
- Children finish picnicking, then pick numerous bouquets. Still, many flowers remain.
- One little girl is so absorbed in the flowers that she doesn't notice how far she has wandered or where.
- She suddenly realizes she's at Goblin Combe, where her mom has said to never go.
- The girl sobs; the fairies hear her.
- They recognize her sweetness and that she is as "good as gold."
- They give her a golden ball and lead her home.
- Rumors of her gift spread.
- There's a miser who spends his days counting gold and always wants more.
- The miser hears the rumors and wants all the fairy's gold.
- He hurries to the forest and picks all the remaining flowers.
- He barges into the fairy cave and is never seen again.

Generosity Bends
the Road

*This true story from Sudan emphasizes the power of gener-
osity and offers insight into the culture of generosity that
continues to thrive there today. I wonder how many other
roads have been, or will be, rerouted in a similar way.*

ABOUT TWO HUNDRED YEARS AGO in Sudan, a man named
Attay lived far off in the countryside. He lived there with his
wife, his seven sons and their wives, his nine daughters and their
husbands, plus sixty-three of his grand-children and great-
grandchildren—some of whom were married. The family on its
own was an entire a village.

Life was good for Attay and all his offspring.

They were able to grow or hunt the food they needed, water in
the river was plentiful, and there were trees and wood enough to
build and heat their homes.

Now and then, they traveled the long road into the city to
trade some of their goods for treats like sugar or ready-made cloth.
But mostly, they stayed home and enjoyed life there.

The village was situated next to the river and far from the caravan road. It was very rare for visitors to come by.

But one day, not far from the village, a caravan of a dozen
merchants lost their way. Many days passed as the men wandered

about. The forest was dense, and they couldn't tell where to go. Sometimes they circled back to where they'd been before. They were growing increasingly worried.

Finally, very early one morning, the merchants awoke to the sound of roosters crowing. It was at some distance and like music to their ears!

They saddled up their camels and loaded their belongings as quickly as they could. By the time they mounted, they could hear the faint sound of dogs barking. More music!

They moved toward the sounds; by sunrise, they could see faint lines of smoke rising into the sky. It could only be a village!

They urged their camels on.

When at last they arrived in the village, they were met by several young men.

The men were smiling and welcomed them warmly. They guided the merchants into a yard where they tied the camels and offered them grass, grain, and water.

The merchants were invited into another yard and welcomed by an elderly man—none other than Attay. He joined twelve young men in offering *karama* to each of the merchants.

In Sudan, *karama* is the traditional offering given as thanks to Allah for a wedding celebration, the birth of a child, or the return of a loved one who has been gone a long time. It is also the traditional offering to a guest. In the old days, as in this story, karama was a sheep that was slaughtered to feed the guest, or for Allah to feed the poor. Today it is still often a sheep, but it might also be some other kind of food like cooked millet or sorghum.

Attay and his family offered karama to each and every one of the twelve merchants, in the form of twelve sheep. According to tradition, the merchants each jumped over their karama sheep. After that, the feasting and celebrations began. The villagers and their guests shared food and stories and songs, praising and glorifying Allah and the Prophet (Peace Be Upon Him).

The villagers made the merchants feel at home and welcomed them to stay for several days until they and their camels were well rested. When at last the merchants were ready to resume their journey, they offered Attay gifts. He refused.

The name Attay means giver, and it was his honor and privilege to be able to host the merchants. He invited them to return again and bring other guests with them.

The merchants were appreciative of the fine treatment they had received from Attay and his family. As they continued their travels, they spoke highly of the experience. They remembered the standing invitation, and within the year, they returned with more men.

Their reception was as warm and as generous as it had been the first time.

After that, stories of Attay and his family spread like fire in dry grass.

Anyone traveling along the caravan road turned off to visit.

Year after year, more and more people came.

Finally, the stream of visitors was so frequent that the route to Attay's village became more visible and distinct than the main caravan road. The former route all but disappeared.

The village of Attay came to be the most important station along the caravan route. All who stopped by were served with the same generosity as the first visiting merchants. All the food and any supplies they needed, a room to sleep, and care for their camels were provided at no cost.

Attay came to be called Awaq Addarib—the one who bent the road. His story is shared to this day in Sudan. The Sudanese continue to offer the same kind of generosity to strangers.

I wonder how many roads have been bent in this way and whether we might be able to bend one too?

FOR REFLECTION

- When have you noticed a dramatic or unforeseen change as a result of generosity?
- What were some of Attay's rewards for his generosity?
- What are some of the rewards you have experienced for your generosity?

THEMES

caring, community, compassion, connection, culture, friendship, generosity, gratitude, history, hospitality, kindness, relationships, service, tradition, wealth

PRINCIPLE

- World community with peace, liberty, and justice for all

STORY MAP

- In Sudan, Attay lives far off the beaten track.
- Attay's extended family is so large it makes a whole village.
- Life is good, with all the necessities available.
- The family rarely travels and visitors seldom come.
- Twelve merchants get lost in the thick forest for several days.
- One morning, they hear roosters crowing and feel hopeful.
- They load their camels and follow the sounds toward the smoke they see rising.
- They are greeted warmly and their camels are cared for.
- Attay and his sons offer karama sheep that the merchants jump over.
- They feast and share stories, songs, and prayers for several days.
- Attay refuses gifts from his guests; instead he invites the merchants to return and bring friends.
- The merchants tell stories of Attay, and eventually they return with friends.
- Rumors of Attay's generosity spread further.

- The village becomes the most important station on the caravan road and the route to the village becomes the main road.
- Attay is renamed "Awaq Addarib," which means the one who bent the road.
- The story lives on in Sudan, as does its spirit of generosity.

The Drum

When given with love, even the most humble offering can have a profound impact on the giver and the recipient alike. In this beautiful Indian story, we are reminded of generosity and how having clarity about the gift we seek can help us find it. Vocal "drumming" helps bring the story to life. You might involve the audience by inviting them to join you on the "tira kita ta dha" refrain. To get the feel of it, you could listen to a tabla *recording.*

WHEN WE GIVE A GIFT, whether it be a small present for our children, financial aid to a worthy cause, or a piece of wisdom that we share, we never quite know what will come of that gift. Let me give you an example. This is a story from India.

tira kita ta dha

tira kita ta dha

> [*Use your hands like a conductor to encourage listeners to join in as you repeat the sounds a few more times.*]

Once, in India, there was a boy who wanted nothing more than to have a drum. His mother wanted nothing more than to give him one. But though she worked long and hard every day, she couldn't afford to buy him one. She could barely afford to buy the food they needed.

One day as she walked home after many long, hard hours selling her grains at the market, she felt especially sorrowful that she couldn't give her son what he wanted. As she walked, a stick caught her eye. She bent down to pick it up, and when she got home, she gave it to her son saying, "This is for you. It's the best I can give you. I wish it were a drum."

The boy was happy with the stick, "Thank you, Amma!" he said, and immediately he began to tap his stick on a pot in their yard.

tira kita ta dha
tira kita ta dha

He hit the fence as he walked by and carried on down the road, dancing to his drum beat. Before long he came upon a neighbor who sat outside by her cooking fire, with tears streaming down her face.

"What's wrong?" asked the boy, full of concern.

"It's my fire. My wood is too wet and I can't light it."

The boy looked at his stick. It was dry. He gave it to the woman. Her fire flared up immediately, and before long she was able to bake the *naan* bread she'd prepared. She thanked the boy and gave him a loaf.

"Thank you!" said the boy. But he wasn't hungry, so he waved the naan a little as he walked, in time to the drumbeats that continued in his head.

tira kita ta dha
tira kita ta dha

Before long, he came to the potter's house. Outside, the baby was wailing.

"Whatever is wrong?" asked the boy.

"We haven't sold a single pot this week," answered the baby's mother, "so I haven't been able to buy food."

The boy looked at the naan bread. "Here have this, I'm not hungry," he said. The baby stopped crying, and the woman was so grateful she reached for a pot. "Here, have this one," she said. "No one seems to want to buy large pots these days."

The boy thanked her and hoisted it on to his head to carry it. Now he could tap his drumbeat on the side of the pot as he walked along.

tira kita ta dha

tira kita ta dha

Before long, the boy came to the river where he saw a washerman and woman quarreling.

"Whatever is the matter?" asked the boy.

"We broke our pot! We don't know what to do. Without it, we can't scrub the clothes properly."

The boy looked up at his pot. "Here, take this, I don't need it." The washerman and woman were so grateful they gave him a coat.

It was a beautiful coat, embroidered with designs and inlaid with mirrors. But the boy wasn't cold. He slung it over his shoulder. Now the drumbeats continued in his head again, as he carried along the road.

tira kita ta dha

tira kita ta dha

Before long the boy came to a bridge. He noticed a man shivering beneath the bridge—he had almost no clothes. The man explained that he'd been robbed.

"Please take my coat," said the boy as he gave it to the man.

The man was thrilled. He pointed to his horse that was grazing nearby. I can't ride or care for my horse anymore. Please take it as a token of my gratitude.

The boy was pleased indeed! But he didn't know how to ride a horse, so he led it along the way. Now he could hear his drumbeats in the horse's hoof steps.

tira kita ta dha

tira kita ta dha

Before long, he came to a forest. A bridegroom, his parents, and a group of musicians sat underneath some trees. They looked very unhappy.

"Whatever is wrong?" asked the boy.

"The groom can't go to his wedding unless he rides on horseback. The auspicious hour for the wedding is soon here, but his horse hasn't arrived."

The boy led the horse over. "Please, take mine."

The family was very grateful, "What can we give you in return?"

The boy could see that the musicians had more than one drum. "Might I have one of those?"

"Of course!" they replied.

Now the boy walked home, beating the drum.

tira kita ta dha

tira kita ta dha

"Mother!" he called out, "Look, the stick you gave me has become a drum!"

FOR REFLECTION

- When have you experienced that giving something away has also given you a gift?
- What are some of the most special gifts that you have received?
- Who in your life has helped you find your true gift?

THEMES

acceptance, caring, character, children, choice, community, compassion, empathy, generosity, gratitude, happiness, hope, humility, interdependence, journey, joy, kindness, letting go, playfulness, presence, service, simplicity, success, wealth, worth

PRINCIPLES

- Justice, equity, and compassion in human relations
- Free and responsible search for truth and meaning
- Respect for the interdependent web of all existence

- We never know what can come of a gift we give.
- In India, a boy wishes for a drum.
- His mother wants to buy him one but can't afford to.
- One day, after working at the market, the mother finds a stick.
- She brings it to her son. He is delighted and creates a rhythm with it.
- He walks along, sees a neighbor is upset, and asks why.
- He gives the neighbor the stick for her fire. She gives him *naan* bread.
- He walks along, waving a rhythm with the naan. He sees a baby crying and asks why.
- The baby is hungry. He gives her the naan bread. The baby's mother gives him a large pot.
- He walks along, tapping a rhythm on the pot. He sees a washer couple arguing and asks why.
- Their wash pot is broken, so he gives them his. They give him a coat.
- He walks along waving the coat in rhythm. He sees a man shivering and asks why.
- The man has been robbed and is cold. The boy gives the man his coat and the man gives the boy his horse.
- The horse walks to the rhythm. The boy sees a wedding party (including the musicians) looking dismayed and asks why.
- The groom needs a horse. The boy gives his horse to the family. They ask what the boy would like.
- The boy sees that the musicians have two drums and asks for one.
- He goes home very happy to tap out a rhythm on his drum.
- His mother rejoices.

Seeking Justice

The Gentleman
and the Thief

This intriguing Chinese story calls to mind the positive result that can come of having faith in and being generous with others. The roles we play need not be permanent; profound transformation is possible.

THE GENTLEMAN WHO WAS CELEBRATING his seventieth birthday was well known for his kind heart and honesty. Guests came from far and wide to honor their noble friend.

In the hubbub of it all, a thief slipped in through the doors. He weaseled his way down the corridor through the crowds, carefully disappearing behind doors or pillars when anyone came too close. His face was well known—he was a wanted man—and he was worried that he'd be recognized.

It wasn't difficult to find the servants' staircase. Using it, he made his way to the upper floor above the main gathering hall and was able to creep along an open ceiling beam, unseen. There he lay, with a perfect overview of the festivities.

He watched as each guest came forward to greet the gentleman and present him with a gift. The old man opened the packages and, after thanking each guest with sincere appreciation, he displayed the gift on one table or another.

The meticulous placement of each gift held the thief's attention. He was keeping careful track of where the most costly items were placed. Once the party was over and the household had gone to bed, the thief planned to retrieve as much gold, silver, silk, and jade as he could carry. He wouldn't waste time with wooden carvings or satin goods, only the best for a thief like him!

Several hours later when the last guest had finally departed, the gentleman lingered for a short time in the room. He continued to rearrange the gifts with a broad smile on his face. It had been a fine party!

The thief shifted to get a better view.

The gentleman noticed the shadow move but did not let on. He organized his gifts for a few more minutes, then called for his servant to set a place for one and bring a meal with the finest of foods.

Both the servant and the thief wondered how the old man could be hungry after his sumptuous birthday feast.

The servant soon returned with the meal. The gentleman dismissed him for the evening, and when he was certain that the entire household had retired, the gentleman looked up toward the roof beam and bowed as though addressing a noble: "Sir, on the roof beam, please come down and enjoy the fine meal that has been set for you."

The thief's cheeks burned a bright red. He had no choice but to accept the invitation and so he climbed down. The gentleman led him to the table and served his meal.

When the thief had eaten his fill, the gentleman bowed down again. He presented the thief with a large bag of silver coins and said, "Sir, I wish you well on your way. These coins are for you to put to good use."

The bag was heavy! The thief could not believe his luck.

Ten years went by, and now the gentleman was celebrating his eightieth birthday. On this auspicious occasion, there were even more family members and guests who came to honor him. His son greeted people as they arrived at the door.

Eventually, a man whom the son did not recognize appeared. He carried an exquisitely wrapped parcel and was adamant that he knew the gentleman. The son ushered him in.

"It is so good to see you in fine health," said the guest.

The gentleman could not recognize the man. "My eyesight is failing. Please, tell me your name."

"I come bearing many gifts—I am an honest man," said the guest.

"Perhaps you'll know me better if I tell you that things weren't always as they are for me now."

The gentleman's curiosity was piqued. "Tell me more!"

The guest continued, "Whereas most of my money once came from shall-we-say questionable sources, and whereas I once squandered it all on one indulgence after another, a stranger's kindness changed everything for me.

"That act of kindness made it impossible for me to go on with my dishonest and selfish ways. I was inspired to be kind to others.

"To my great surprise, I found myself treating my elders with courtesy and respect. When someone came collecting alms, I gave generously. I opened my door to strangers. The pleasure it brought amazed me! I felt more contentment and harmony than ever before."

The guest was now almost whispering as he continued, "The strange thing is, these acts of kindness seemed also to bring more wealth. I am not as rich as you my noble lord, but I have come to know more riches than ever before. I hope you will accept my gift."

The gentleman had a twinkle in his eye as he said, "But your name. I cannot accept a gift unless I know who it is from."

The guest replied, "You could address me in this way: 'Sir, on the roof beam, please come down and enjoy the fine meal that has been set for you.'"

The gentleman smiled broadly, embraced his guest warmly, and welcomed him to the feast.

He marveled at the fine gemstone his guest had brought, and as he placed it at the center of the gift table, he said, "Your story is as true a gift as the stone. I humbly thank you for both."

FOR REFLECTION

- How has another person's generosity changed you?
- When has changing something that you do changed how you feel about yourself and who you are?
- We often say that "we can only change ourselves," but what are some ways that another person has helped you change?

THEMES

acceptance, belief, caring, change, character, choice, class, compassion, connection, conscience, dignity, discernment, education, empathy, equality, ethics, evil, faith, forgiveness, freedom, generosity, gratitude, greed, growth, guilt, honesty, hope, hospitality, humility, identity, inclusion, integrity, intuition, justice, kindness, mentorship, money, non-violence, reconciliation, redemption, respect, self-respect, success, transcendence, transformation, trust, vision, wholeness

PRINCIPLES

- Inherent worth and dignity of every person
- Justice, equity, and compassion in human relations
- Acceptance of one another and encouragement to spiritual growth
- Free and responsible search for truth and meaning
- World community with peace, liberty, and justice for all

- A noble gentleman celebrates his seventieth birthday. Many guests attend the party.
- A thief slips in and hides on the roof beam.
- The thief notes where the costly gifts are placed.
- When the last guest has left, the gentleman sees the thief's shadow.
- The gentleman calls for his servant to bring dinner for one.
- He invites "Sir on the roof beam" to enjoy the meal.
- The thief is embarrassed but accepts, feeling he has no choice.
- After the meal, the gentleman gives the thief a bag of silver "to put to good use."
- Ten years later, the noble gentleman celebrates his eightieth birthday.
- His son welcomes the guests and doesn't recognize one.
- The guest is adamant that he knows the gentleman. The son ushers him in.
- The gentleman feigns poor eyesight when he can't recall the guest's name.
- The guest is evasive about his identity. He tells the story of a stranger's kindness and how it changed him for the better.
- For the first time, he treated elders with respect, gave to the poor, and welcomed strangers.
- The gentleman smiles and insists on knowing the guest's name.
- The guest suggests he be addressed as "Sir on the roof beam."
- The gentleman smiles more. Better than the guest's gift is the guest's story.

The Jug
on the Rock

Compassion and creative thinking are important tools in the administration of justice. In this refreshing story from Tibet, we are reminded not to be too quick in passing judgment, and we see that when a community acts together, it can ease the burden of one of its members.

A MAN CARRIED HIS LARGE CLAY JUG full of freshly made yogurt-milk.

He walked the streets of town, calling out, "Dara for sale! Dara for sale!"

People opened their doors with pitchers in their hands. The milkman filled their pitchers from his own larger vessel and happily accepted their payment. He was a good man who shared his profits with his elderly mother even as he cared for his own family.

By noon, the milkman was always ready for a rest.

One day, he set the jug down on a big rock and found a nearby rock for himself. He savored the momo dumplings that his wife had packed for his lunch. He could hear the wind whistling and goats bleating.

A loud voice called, "Ta-shee-day-lay!" or "Hello!" It was a shepherd.

[*You might take time to teach your audience "ta-shee-day-lay," and involve them in saying it when it's repeated later in the story.*]

The milkman replied with an equally loud, "Ta-shee-day-lay!" The sudden sound of his voice startled one of the goats. The goat jumped up and bumped into the jug.

"Crash!" The jug fell off its rock and broke.

"My jug!" groaned the milkman. "Your goat broke my jug. You must pay for it!"

The shepherd had no money to spare. Just like the milkman, he shared everything with his elderly mother, even as he looked after his family. He replied, "You shouldn't have perched it like that on the rock. It's your own fault!"

The two men argued back and forth all afternoon. They could not agree on who should take the blame and pay to replace the jug. Finally they decided to take the case to court.

Together, they walked up the path to the village square that was just outside the temple, where a monk could always be found. Monks were the ones who dispensed justice in those days and considered cases such as this one. The men bowed before the monk and asked to tell their story.

The monk listened carefully and, rubbing his chin, said, "The milkman could have been more careful with his jug, and yet it is not his fault that it broke. Without it, he cannot earn what he needs to care for his family or his elderly mother. It was the goat, not the shepherd, who broke the jug. If the shepherd were to pay for it, he would have to sell his goats and then he would not be able to earn what he needs to care for his family or his elderly mother."

He continued, "If neither of the men are to blame, then it must be the fault of the goat and the rock. They are the ones who must be tried."

135

The goat came willingly. But it took twenty men to carry the rock into the village square.

By then, the entire village had heard about the disagreement and many had come to watch the proceedings. At first the square resounded with the sound of people greeting one another, [*Put your hand to your ear, and help people repeat "ta-shee-day-lay."*] As they talked together, more and more people began to snicker and scorn the proceedings. Some shouted, "This is ridiculous."

Finally, the monk looked up to acknowledge the crowd that had gathered. He scolded, "Do you really think I am going to apply the law to a rock and a goat? Do you take me for a fool? Or are you here to mock our laws?"

When he could see that his words had sunk in, the monk began to smile, "Each and every one of you who is laughing is guilty of improper thought. The fine is one *gyatso*, one copper coin."

The monk held out his hands. [*You might do this, with a big smile, and pretend to collect coins from your audience.*] For a moment, people stared in disbelief. Slowly, one then another reached into their pockets and their purses to extract the small coin. A single gyatso meant little to them.

Each of them placed their coin in the monk's open hands. Soon he held a large collection of coins.

The monk turned to the grief-stricken milkman, "This should be plenty for you to buy a new jug."

Most of the crowd began to smile.

And the next day, the milkman could be heard calling, "Dara for sale! Dara for sale!"

Customers everywhere called out in greeting. [*Put your hand to your ear, and help people repeat "ta-shee-day-lay."*]

FOR REFLECTION

- What is the importance of imagination and good humor in resolving situations like this?
- When have you been prompted to think outside the box, and what has helped you do that?
- When have you used or experienced humor as a tool to inspire action?
- When have the people around you supported you through a challenge?

THEMES

anger, authority, blame, choice, community, compassion, compromise, conflict, covenant, creativity, dignity, empathy, ethics, generosity, governance, guilt, hope, imagination, justice, leadership, listening, money, peace, playfulness, poverty, reconciliation, responsibility, solidarity, suffering, teamwork, work

PRINCIPLES

- Justice, equity, and compassion in human relations
- Right of conscience and use of the democratic process
- World community with peace, liberty, and justice for all

STORY MAP

- In Tibet, the milkman calls, "Dara for sale!" as he carries a large pot of yogurt-milk around the village.
- The man supports his elderly mother and his own family with his earnings.
- He sets his jug on a rock when he takes a break to eat momo.
- He hears a shepherd call "Ta-shee-day-lay!" ("Hello!") and replies.
- His voice startles the shepherd's goat, who jumps up and bumps against the jug.
- It falls off the rock with a crash! The milkman is upset. He has lost his source of income and blames the shepherd.
- The shepherd is an honest man who supports his elderly mother and own family.
- The shepherd can't afford to buy a new jug. He says it's the milkman's own fault.
- They argue back and forth. Finally they agree to go to court.
- The court is next to a temple; the judge is a monk.

- The monk listens carefully and determines that it's neither man's fault.
- He says the fault lies either with the goat or the rock and they must come to court.
- The goat comes easily. Twenty men must carry the rock.
- News about the court case spreads. Many onlookers arrive and begin to mock the proceedings.
- When the monk begins to speak, the people laugh more.
- The monk scolds onlookers and says that each person who laughed is guilty of improper thought and that the fine for this is one gyatso.
- The monk collects the small coins. He sees that the sum is perfect, enough for the milkman to buy a new jug.
- Most of the crowd smiles in understanding.
- The milkman is able to continue his work.

Strength in Unity

With audience participation, the power of working together is brought to life. When I first told this old Indian story, I remembered only the first part and I've shared it that way here. I like that it is short and to the point. In case you are curious about the traditional tale, I provide the Panchatantra and Jataka endings.

A DARK CLOUD OF WORRY spread through the forest. No longer were the hunters satisfied with capturing birds in their snares one at a time.

They had developed a new technology: They were taking long strands of fiber, criss-crossing them one strand over another, and tying the strands fast at those intersections.

Do you know what they were making?

Nets.

Now, instead of capturing a single bird, they could capture a handful, a dozen, or hundreds of them all at once. The birds that escaped this new invention were frightened. What could they do?

Some birds lost all hope.

"It's pointless," they peeped, with feeble voices. "There's no way we can escape this horror. We might as well give up right now."

Others got busy, building up their muscle strength and sharpening their bills.

"If I get caught," boasted those birds, "I'll be able to cut my way free. I'll be strong enough to fly away."

It was encouraging to hear hope, but not all of the birds liked the brazen approach of the strong birds. Some of the birds said, "If I escape while others die, my life will be filled with unhappiness."

A meeting was called. The birds talked back and forth:

Caw-caw-caw,

Te-whit, te-whoo,

Chickadee-dee-dee,

Cuckoo-cuckoo.

[*You might put your hand on your ear to invite
listeners to offer other calls.*]

At last, the birds had a plan. And sure enough, it wasn't long before they had a chance to test it.

Peep. Peep. Many birds heard the call. A call of distress. Who was it?

Birds of all shape and size flew toward the sound. They landed on the branches of a big tree. But where was the injured bird? They couldn't see it.

Suddenly, they were trapped beneath a net. It was a trick! And now, they could barely move.

Some of the birds panicked, and cried out.

But others remained calm. Soon a whisper ran through the flock of birds that had been caught.

"Take a deep breath. Remember our plan. When the king of birds sings, let us all flap our wings." The whisper was repeated, and soon it resounded from one end of the net to the other.

"Take a deep breath. Remember our plan. When the king of birds sings, let us all flap our wings."

The birds breathed in.

The king whistled a plaintive note: whhhhhhhhh.

[*You might put your hand on your ear to invite
a listener to whistle.*]

The birds began to flap their wings.

[*You might invite listeners to flap their "wings," being careful
of their neighbors. Model flapping wings to them, first with
difficulty, and then with greater ease.*]

It was hard work!

When it began to feel impossible for some of the birds, they looked over at their neighbors, who were also hard at work, and felt encouraged. They continued to flap their wings.

Suddenly, they lifted right out of that tree. They rose higher and higher into the sky, carrying the net with them.

The king whistled a plaintive note once more: whhhhhhhhh. The birds tilted their bodies to the side in unison, as though they were one. The net slid off their backs and dropped to the ground.

After that, a new melody could be heard in the forest: "There's strength in unity. There's strength in unity."

That is the story of how the birds met their worst fears.

It is the story of how we can meet ours.

Panchatantra Ending

The birds alighted together on another tree, but couldn't free themselves from the net. Again, the king remained calm. Now he called for his friend Mouse.

"Please, Mouse, will you set us free?" Mouse agreed and immediately began to chew at the net next to the king.

"No, no, no! You must set the others free first!"

"It is only right if I release you, the king of all birds, first."

"But I won't be truly free unless my subjects are also free."

The mouse nibbled at the net with its sharp teeth. Once he had set all the other birds free, he released the king. The birds were happy to stretch their wings once more!

Before flying off home, they bowed together in gratitude to their friend the mouse.

Jataka Ending

The birds escape from the hunter several times, but eventually an argument breaks out amongst them and in their distraction, without clear leadership, they are captured.

FOR REFLECTION

- What are some of the benefits of working together?
- What makes cooperation and collaboration difficult at times?
- What would be different if the birds did not have a strong leader? How might they have succeeded without one?
- What are some important qualities of a true leader?

THEMES

activism, anti-oppression, commitment, community, courage, covenant, creativity, faith, fear, freedom, generosity, hope, interdependence, leadership, limitations, power, responsibility, solidarity, strength, teamwork, unity, vision, weakness, worth

PRINCIPLES

- Inherent worth and dignity of every person
- Right of conscience and use of the democratic process
- World community with peace, liberty, and justice for all

STORY MAP

- Worry spreads amongst the forest birds.
- Hunters have a new technology. Using nets, they can capture dozens of birds at once.
- The birds are frightened. Some lose all hope; others work to protect themselves; others say it's wrong to consider only their own safety.

142

- A meeting is held.
- A plan is made and very soon is tested.
- A bird calls out in distress. When several birds rush to help, all are trapped in a net.
- Some panic; others remember the plan.
- The king of birds whistles to signal for all birds to flap their wings.
- They do so and rise together into the sky, lifting the net.
- The king whistles again. All tilt to one side and the net slips off.
- The birds sing together, and it sounds like "strength in unity."

Sister Goose
and the Foxes

This Texan story of Sister Goose presents a bleak truth about corruption amongst the people in power and the system in place. Pairing it with the story that follows, "Brother Fox and the Geese," is a satisfying way of offering critique of the justice system and hope for change.

SISTER GOOSE SWAM IN THE POND, happy as could be. Now and then, she ducked her head down to nibble a little bit here, and a little bit there. She took no more than her fill of those succulent underwater plants, for she knew that the pond belonged to everyone.

Meanwhile, Brother Fox was hiding in the willows at the far end of the pond. He didn't like to see anyone happy, least of all a goose.

Sister Goose swam along, enjoying the clear blue sky and the bright sunshine. She swam along to the willows growing at the far end of the pond. All of a sudden Brother Fox sprang right out of those willows shouting, "Trespasser! You get off my lake!"

Sister Goose shrugged up her wings and looked at Brother Fox, mystified. "Trespasser? How so? This lake does not belong to you, it belongs to us all!"

144

Brother Fox didn't seem to hear her. He carried on, "You've been eating some of the plants in this pond. They don't belong to you! If you don't get out of this lake, I'm going to take you to court!"

Sister Goose was truly perplexed. She knew she hadn't done anything wrong, but she could see by the ugly gleam in Brother Fox's eyes that she would not be able to convince him of that. Instead she said, "I'm not afraid to go to court over this. At least there, justice will be served."

And so they went to court.

But when Sister Goose arrived at the courthouse, she was very surprised. The clerks who sat just inside the doors were both foxes. Inside the courtroom, she saw that the lawyers were foxes. And the judge was a fox. And even the jurymen, though some of them had red fur and some of them had brown fur and some of them had silver fur, were all foxes too.

Sister Goose was quaking as she entered the defendant's booth. Sure enough, though her arguments were sound, the judge and the jury found her guilty. They convicted her and turned her into stew.

That is how it goes. There isn't much justice for the likes of a goose when the folks in the courthouse are all foxes.

FOR REFLECTION

- When, in your experience, has justice seemed impossible?
- Who are today's foxes? Who are today's geese?
- What examples do you know of the "geese" winning?

THEMES

anti-oppression, authority, class, courage, culture, equality, ethics, evil, freedom, governance, history, human rights, identity, justice, oppression, power, privilege, race/ethnicity, rights, strength, suffering, violence, vulnerability, weakness

PRINCIPLES

- Inherent worth and dignity of every person
- Justice, equity, and compassion in human relations
- Right of conscience and use of the democratic process
- World community with peace, liberty, and justice for all

STORY MAP

- Sister Goose is swimming and dining in the lake.
- Brother Fox demands that she leave because the public lake is his property.
- Sister Goose refuses to leave.
- An argument ensues between Sister Goose and Brother Fox.
- They agree to settle in court.
- On the day of the trial, the clerk, the lawyers, the jury, and the judge are all foxes.
- Sister Goose is found guilty and eaten.

Brother Fox
and the Geese

*This story affirms that standing together can help us over-
come an unfair system. It is based on a Grimm Brothers' tale
and offers a good antidote to the previous one, "Sister Goose
and the Fox." I like to tell them together, ending on a positive
note with this one. When linking this story with the previous
one, you might want to begin with "Meanwhile . . ."*

IT WAS MID-MORNING. Sister Goose and all her extended family
were feasting. She and her brothers, her sisters, her cousins, her
aunts, and her uncles had come upon a gorgeous meadow full of
lush green grass and plump ripe grains. Yummy!

They ate so much that their stomachs swelled right up until
they almost touched the ground. They were so full they could
barely move.

Meanwhile, Brother Fox was out walking. It seemed like forever
since he had last eaten, and his stomach was rumbling. As he came
around a curve in the path, his nose twitched a little. Something
smelled very sweet. He walked a little further and, sure enough,
there in the meadow were more geese than he could count. He
began to salivate.

He snuck his way in amongst the tall grass, but quiet as he was, he couldn't fool the geese. They caught sight of his great big teeth and his long sharp claws.

Some of those geese began to quiver and quake. Some began to cry. Some hid their heads under their wings.

Sister Goose was just as worried as the rest of them. She knew that there was no escape. The meadow, except for the path where Brother Fox stood, was surrounded on all sides by a tall cliff. And they were too full to fly.

Sister Goose quivered and quaked, but then she took a deep breath in. She wasn't going to give in or give up!

Sister Goose took in another deep breath and then she called out, "Before you eat us, please let us say one last prayer."

Brother Fox salivated some more. He thought that with a little spiritual sustenance, the geese might taste even sweeter. He said, "You go ahead and say your last prayer while I choose the plumpest among you."

Sister Goose held her wings out to her brothers, her sisters, her cousins, her aunts, and her uncles. Pretty soon the geese were all holding wings in a great big circle. They began to pray, "Gaggle, gaggle, gaggle."

The geese continued to pray, "Gaggle, gaggle, gaggle."

[*You might motion for the audience to join you in the actions. Be sure to plan how you'll get them to stop so you can finish the story.*]

Their prayers were rhythmic. They were harmonic. They inspired the geese to dance a little. They kept right on praying, "Gaggle, gaggle, gaggle."

Finally, Brother Fox fell asleep.

By then, the geese had digested their feast and were able to walk around the sleeping fox.

While he snored, his teeth didn't look near so sharp nor his claws near so long.

FOR REFLECTION

- When have you experienced the power of solidarity?
- What are some sources of inspiration for acting together?
- What are some situations that might be benefitted by greater solidarity?

THEMES

activism, anti-oppression, authority, choice, class, commitment, community, courage, covenant, creativity, dignity, evil, faith, fear, history, hope, human rights, interdependence, leadership, non-violence, patience, power, race/ethnicity, rights, solidarity, spiritual practice, spirituality, strength, teamwork, transcendence, unity, violence, vision, vulnerability, weakness

PRINCIPLES

- Acceptance of one another and encouragement to spiritual growth
- The right of conscience and the use of the democratic process
- World community with peace, liberty, and justice for all

STORY MAP

- A flock of geese are feeding in a meadow.
- They have eaten too much and are too full to fly.
- A fox approaches and threatens to eat them.
- The meadow is surrounded by cliffs. The geese realize there's no escape.
- The geese beg permission for a final prayer. The fox allows it.
- The geese hold wings in a circle and begin to pray. They continue praying, singing, dancing, shouting, and holding wings.
- The fox falls asleep.
- With all of the movement, the geese have now digested their food and can escape the fox.

Two Pebbles

Faith, when coupled with creative thinking, can help solve even the most difficult problems. The story stands perfectly well on its own, but because it adds another perspective on justice and empowerment, I've often told it between the previous Fox and Goose stories. Originally, this story featured a girl, her father, and their landlord, but to tie the three stories together, I retell it as another Fox and Goose tale. This particular story is sometimes identified as Chinese and sometimes as Indian, but there are very similar stories from all around the world of a wise child helping her father out of a tricky situation.

DADDY GOOSE and Daughter Goose lived in the cutest little house. Daughter Goose loved it when her daddy stayed home. They'd play games and tell stories; they'd sing songs and paint pictures.

But of course Daddy Goose needed to work. He worked most days. He worked long and hard. Even so, some months when Mister Fox came knocking at the door with his paw outstretched, it was difficult to find enough money to pay the rent.

One month, when Mister Fox came, Daddy Goose did not have enough money. He begged for a little more time.

"One day," said Mister Fox, "that is what I'll give you. One more day to pay the rent."

Daddy Goose fretted as he hurried out the door to find work. Daughter Goose comforted him, "Don't worry Daddy, we'll find a way."

The next day when Mister Fox came knocking, Daddy Goose was away working to earn the money they needed. Daughter Goose was home alone painting pictures. She stepped outside and apologized sweetly: "My Daddy will be back soon. Why don't we play a game to pass the time?" She had suspected that Mister Fox loved a good game. And she was right.

His eyes lit up. "Well all right" he said. "What kind of game?"

"I don't know," said Daughter Goose. "You can choose."

And then she added, "But if I win, I get to choose how much rent to pay. If you win, you get to choose."

"But you'll choose not to pay." protested Mister Fox.

"Exactly," said Daughter Goose. "I'll choose not to pay rent for the whole entire year."

"Well then," said Mister Fox, "If I win, I'll choose . . . I'll choose . . . triple the rent!"

Daughter Goose gasped. She hadn't meant for the stakes to get that high, but now it was too late.

Mister Fox said, "We can play a simple sort of game. I'll pick up a black pebble and a white pebble." He placed one in each paw and closed them tight. "You choose which paw. If you choose the one with the white pebble, you win. But if you choose the one with the black pebble, I win."

Daughter Goose gulped as she nodded in agreement to the rules of the game. Then she watched Mister Fox bend down to pick up the two pebbles, and saw, to her horror, that he picked up two black pebbles. He closed his paws around them.

What to do? Whichever paw she chose, she'd lose. *Or would she?*

Daughter Goose was worried, but she reminded herself that she often won games. She stayed calm as she looked back and forth at his two paws. She stretched her wing out beneath the left one. "Drop the pebble!"

Mister Fox smiled as he let the pebble fall.

What color was it?

Black, of course, but oops! Somehow, it slipped right between Daughter Goose's feathers and dropped to the ground.

"I'm so sorry! Silly me!" exclaimed Daughter Goose. Both could see that there was no hope of finding the pebble on the ground—there were too many black and white pebbles there already!

"I have a solution Mister Fox," said Daughter Goose, "If you'll kindly show me the pebble in your other paw, we'll both know which one you dropped."

Old Mr. Fox knew that he was trapped. He snarled as he opened his fist to reveal the remaining pebble.

What color was it?

Black, of course. And so *what color was the one he'd dropped*?

It must have been white! There was no denying that Daughter Goose had won the game. A deal was a deal, and Mister Fox had no choice but to agree that a year would go by before he'd be back to collect the rent. He stomped off.

Daughter Goose couldn't wait to tell her daddy that he would be able stay home to play games, tell stories, sing songs, and paint pictures with her a little more often in the coming year.

———————

FOR REFLECTION

- When has quick thinking served you well?
- What helps you think laterally, like the daughter in this story?

- In what ways do you relate to Daddy or Daughter Goose?
- When have you been aware of someone trying to offer "two black pebbles"?

THEMES

anti-oppression, authority, choice, class, courage, creativity, dignity, discernment, equality, ethics, evil, fear, greed, honesty, hope, human rights, integrity, intuition, justice, money, poverty, presence, privilege, reason, trust, truth

PRINCIPLES

- Justice, equity, and compassion in human relations
- The right of conscience and the use of the democratic process
- World community with peace, liberty, and justice for all

STORY MAP

- Daddy Goose and his daughter love to play.
- Daddy must work long and hard to earn enough money.
- One month he doesn't have the rent money when it's due and begs for more time.
- Mr. Fox, the landlord, gives one day only.
- Daddy Goose is worried. His daughter has faith that things will work out.
- Mr. Fox comes to collect the rent while Daddy Goose is away working.
- Daughter Goose apologizes and suggests they play a game to pass the time.
- She offers Mr. Fox his choice of games. They agree that the winner will decide the amount of the rent.
- If Daughter Goose wins, she and her father will get a year rent-free. If Mr. Fox wins, he will triple the rent.
- Mr. Fox suggests a game with black and white pebbles in which Daughter Goose must pick the hand holding the white pebble.
- Daughter Goose sees Mr. Fox pick up two black pebbles. It seems she will lose whichever hand she chooses.
- With faith, Daughter Goose holds out her wing.
- When Mr. Fox releases the pebble, she "accidentally" drops it.
- There are so many pebbles on the ground that it's impossible to discern which one was dropped.

153

- Daughter Goose tells Mr. Fox to open his other hand. The pebble is black, and therefore he "must have" dropped the white pebble.
- Mr. Fox is outraged but can't argue. Daughter Goose wins a year of no rent.
- Daughter Goose can't wait to tell her daddy they'll have more time to play.

The Bell of Justice

For a long time, people have argued that in a truly just system, no one is above or below the law. This story about fair treatment is drawn from Henry Wadsworth Long- fellow's poem, which was based on a story from Gesta Romanorum, *a Latin language collection that was com- piled toward the end of the thirteenth century. The story is also found in Burma and Russia.*

RE GIOVANNI OF ABRUZZO, Italy, was a good and wise king. There was nothing he wanted more for his kingdom than for it to be famous for its justice. To that end, he built a great bell tower in the center of town, and in it, he hung a beautiful brass bell with a long hemp cord attached as its pull.

Imagine, for a moment, the sound of that bell.

> [*You might smile to your audience and put your hand to your ear to encourage them to provide a ringing sound, now and at other times in the story when the bell rings.*]

Re Giovanni sent riders throughout the land to proclaim to all his citizens that justice would be served. Anyone who felt they had been mistreated was invited to ring the bell. When it rang, the king could hear it, no matter where he was. And when he heard it ring out he would summon his judges to hear the case.

At first, the bell rang loudly and often: when a neighbor was greedy, or when a thief came visiting, or when a dispute could not be settled. The judges gathered to listen and consider every case that came before them. Justice was served. Abruzzo grew famous as a land of equity and fairness. The king and his people relaxed and became so accustomed to the justice of the land that they didn't notice when the bell cord grew worn and thin.

Finally, little was left of the cord but tatters. It might have disappeared completely except that a vine attached itself to the cord and began to grow.

But let us return for a moment to the time when the tower was being built. There was a soldier who was young and full of idealism. He mounted his horse and traveled out into the world to offer his services far and wide. He and his horse were skilled at war; together they earned the soldier both fame and fortune.

By the time the vine had wound itself around the bell cord, the soldier had grown old. By then, he had returned to retire high up on a hill in a grand estate.

There, he felt himself above the affairs of state and above the law. He was interested in little else but his gold. Even more than everyone else, he had forgotten about the bell tower and its cord. Day in, day out, the old soldier counted his gold. He gloated over the piles of coins and loved how they gleamed.

He was so pre-occupied with his good fortune that he forgot his faithful horse. She had carried him into many battles and saved his life more than once, but now that the mare was old and lame, the soldier was too stingy to feed her. Instead, he let her loose to find her own food.

It didn't take long before the horse had devoured the small amount of sweet grass that grew on the hillside. She wandered further afield, finding little to eat. Her skin sagged, her back swayed, her bones ached, and her stomach growled.

One day when she was close to town, the mare's nose twitched. She smelled something green and fresh. She followed the scent into the town square. The luscious smell was none other than the vine that now grew from the bell of justice.

The horse began to gnaw on the vine. She was so hungry that she didn't notice that, with every bite she took, the bell rang. She was so hungry that the bell of justice rang out over and over.

The villagers heard it, the judges heard it, and the old king heard it. Soon the square was full of curious onlookers, who became all the more curious when they saw that there was no man nor woman near the bell tower. Instead, it was a scrawny old horse ringing the bell of justice.

One after another, they recognized that the horse belonged to the old soldier on the hill. Soon the square was filled with murmurs about the treatment the soldier was giving his faithful mare. How, they wondered, could he have allowed her to decline into such rough shape?

When the soldier heard his summons, he laughed. What foolishness was this? How could a hero such as himself be called a criminal?

But when he arrived in the square, he found it full of outraged men and women who made it clear that he had lost their respect.

The soldier went home, with his tail between his legs, to fetch some of his precious gold to pay the fine, and pay for proper food and care for his faithful horse.

The king had that bell cord restored.

It would remind the soldier, and everyone else, that no one, not the rich or the famous or even the heroic, are above the bell of justice. No person or animal is beneath being served by that bell. Let it ring on!

———

FOR REFLECTION

- Is there a time when you have felt moved to ring "the bell of justice"?
- What was the impact of ringing that bell, on yourself and others?
- What kinds of measures are necessary for justice to prevail?

THEMES

activism, aging, animals, anti-oppression, arrogance, authority, caring, change, class, community, covenant, dignity, dissent, equality, ethics, governance, greed, history, human rights, identity, inclusion, justice, leadership, listening, power, privilege, responsibility, rights, suffering, truth, vulnerability, weakness, worth

PRINCIPLES

- Inherent worth and dignity of every person
- Justice, equity, and compassion in human relations
- Right of conscience and the use of the democratic process
- World community with peace, liberty, and justice for all

STORY MAP

- The good and wise king wants to ensure there is justice in the land.
- A bell tower is built. The bell has a long hemp cord that is accessible to all who seek justice.
- When the bell is rung, the case is heard.
- At first, the bell rings often. Many cases are heard.
- Eventually there is less crime and less need for the bell.
- No one notices that the cord wears thin or that a vine grows around it.
- At the time the bell of justice is installed, a young man becomes a skilled soldier.
- The soldier earns fame and fortune.
- When the bell cord has worn thin, the soldier returns home.
- He retires in a grand estate on the hill. He is interested only in his gold.
- His faithful horse is now old and he doesn't bother to feed her. The horse must find her own food on the hillside.
- The fodder on the hill is soon gone, and the horse grows skinny and worn.
- The horse catches the scent of the vine and chews on it.

- The bell rings. The villagers, judges, and king are curious.
- All are surprised to see a horse there. They recognize it, and call for the soldier.
- The soldier feels he is above the law but comes.
- The soldier is fined.
- The bell cord is restored. No one is above justice. No creature is beneath justice.

The Fifty-Dollar Bill

We all jump to conclusions at times. This urban legend, known in England and the U.S., warns us to be careful about making assumptions.

AN ELDERLY BROTHER AND SISTER lived together. Neither of them much liked going into town to do the shopping, but now and then, it was a necessary thing.

Usually it was the sister who did the errands, and so it went this time. She bustled about getting ready, and her brother gave her a fifty-dollar bill. "I hope this will be enough."

"Surely it will!" said the sister as she continued to rush about with her preparations. She was worried she might not catch her train. A moment or two later, she was hurrying to the station as quickly as she could.

Her worries were all for naught. Soon enough, she found herself sitting very comfortably and alone in a cozy six-seater section of the coach. The quiet and rhythmic swaying of the train caused her to drift off to sleep.

But not for long. She still had to make her shopping list and plan her errands.

When she opened her eyes, she saw that another passenger had joined her in the six-seat section. She was a little surprised that a grubby looking person like him had enough money for a train ticket. He looked like he hadn't had a bath in ages.

She pulled her bag a little closer, then reached down into it for her small notebook and pen. After working on her list for a few moments, she remembered the fifty-dollar bill her brother had given her. She checked to see that it was safely stowed in her bag.

It wasn't there! Where could it be?

She dug through every corner of her bag, at least twice. She still didn't find the fifty dollars.

She looked suspiciously at her fellow passenger. He was snoring. His bag was within reach.

Surely he hadn't taken her money.

But what if he had? She decided to take a quick peak.

There on the very top of his bag was her fifty-dollar bill!

How outrageous. What audacity!

Should she tell the conductor? Ahhh, it would cause such a stir if she did. And it didn't seem right to embarrass the man. He might get thrown off the train. That would be too much.

No. No. It was better just to take back the money. So she did. She tucked it safely into her wallet and put the wallet deep inside her bag.

Soon enough, they arrived at her stop. The other passenger opened his eyes when she stood up to go.

She wouldn't bear a grudge. She pulled herself together and nodded farewell to the man with a warm smile.

She walked briskly from the train station to the shopping center. In no time at all, her errands were done. After a nice cup of tea, she returned to the station to catch the next train home.

Her brother was reading the newspaper when she arrived. He watched as she unpacked her parcels with a look of surprise on his face. "How did you manage to pay for all of that? I was sure you'd come home empty-handed."

"Why ever would I do that?" asked the woman, a little irritated.

"Your fifty-dollar bill is still sitting on the table."

The woman sat down with a thump.

FOR REFLECTION

- What assumptions have you made that caused you embarrassment? What might you have done differently?
- What might have happened had the woman in the story spoken directly to the stranger on the train? How might she make amends for her mistake?
- What are some tools to help prevent us from making assumptions?

THEMES

anger, anti-oppression, arrogance, assumptions, blame, character, class, conscience, discernment, equality, ethics, failure, greed, guilt, honesty, humility, identity, intuition, justice, money, poverty, privilege, reason, regret, self-respect, shame, trust, wealth

PRINCIPLES

- Inherent worth and dignity of every person
- Justice, equity, and compassion in human relations
- Acceptance of one another and encouragement to spiritual growth
- World community with peace, liberty, and justice for all

STORY MAP

- An elderly brother and sister live together.
- The sister occasionally does their errands in town.
- One day while the sister is busy preparing, the brother puts a fifty-dollar bill on the table and tells her.
- The sister fusses some more and then rushes out the door.
- She hurries to the station and catches the train.
- She relaxes in an otherwise empty six-seat coach and then falls asleep.
- When she wakes up, a scruffy stranger is in one of the seats.

- She begins writing her shopping list. Then she checks for her fifty dollars. The bill is gone!
- The stranger is sleeping. His bag is within reach. She peeks in and sees her bill.
- She is outraged!
- She considers telling the conductor, but she doesn't want to cause embarrassment or trouble.
- She quietly retrieves the money.
- She doesn't bear a grudge and smiles to the stranger as she gets off the train.
- She does the shopping, has tea, and returns home.
- The brother is surprised to see that his sister has been able to buy anything.
- When she wonders why, he explains that the fifty-dollar bill is still on the table.

Developing Perspective

The Magnificent Red Bud Tree

∎ · ∎ · ∎

Our preconceptions and experiences limit our view of the world. Based on a traditional Jataka tale from India, this story reminds us that when we take another person's views into consideration, we can gain a deeper understanding of the whole picture. Note that traditionally, the Buddha (represented by the king) would have solved the puzzle for the princes. I allow the princes and the audience to solve the puzzle themselves.

HAVE YOU EVER KNOWN something, known it really well, and been certain that you're absolutely right?

You're not the first.

Once, there were four princes, brothers, who all their lives had heard stories about a magnificent red bud tree, more marvelous than any other tree. They all wanted to see it, and they all wanted to be the first.

Late one winter, the eldest brother found an opportunity. He was alone in the chariot with the driver when suddenly he thought, "Today's the day!" and so he asked the driver, "Please, will you bring me into the forest to see the red bud tree?"

The driver gasped a little. It was a long and dangerous journey, and yet he understood the boy's desire, and so he agreed. Soon they were winding their way along the narrow, winding track, deeper and deeper into the forest. The chariot stopped. The boy got out. He soon saw the one tree that was different from all the others in the forest canopy.

But the prince was so stunned and disappointed by what he saw that he didn't say a word, not in the forest, nor when he got home. Had his brothers been more observant, they might have noticed a certain new sadness in his demeanor.

A few months later, the second prince found his chance. He was alone in the chariot with the driver and said, "Could we take a detour, to see the red bud tree?"

The driver gasped again. The journey was no less long or dangerous than it had been with the first prince. And yet he had brought the first boy there, and so he agreed again. Soon they were winding their way along that narrow, winding track, deep and deeper into the forest. The chariot stopped. The boy got out and soon recognized the one tree that was different from all the others in the forest canopy.

He was so awed by what he saw that he was speechless. He couldn't sort out what to say and so he didn't say a thing. Had his brothers been more observant, they might have noticed a quiet joyfulness in his demeanor.

Another few months went by when the third prince had his chance. You know what happened. He was alone in the chariot with the driver and he said, "Could we take a detour, and see the red bud tree?"

The driver sighed. The journey was so dangerous and yet it wouldn't be fair not to give the third brother a chance, and so he agreed. [*By now, your audience will be able to help you with the refrain.*] Soon, they were winding their way along that narrow, winding track, deep and deeper into the forest. The driver stopped.

The boy got out and soon recognized the one tree that was different from all the others in the forest canopy.

He was so unpleasantly startled by what he saw that he, too, could not speak, nor did he ask any questions. Again, the other brothers heard nothing of his experience. Had his brothers been more observant, they might have noticed bitterness in his demeanor.

Another few months went by before the fourth, the youngest prince, finally had his chance. You know what happened. He was alone in the chariot with the driver and he said, "Could we take a detour, and see the red bud tree?"

The driver sighed. "Not again!" And yet how could he deny the last brother this opportunity? [*Again, you might invite your audience to join you and support them in providing the refrain.*] Soon, they were winding their way along that narrow, winding track, deep and deeper into the forest. The chariot stopped. The boy got out and soon recognized the one tree that was different from all the others in the forest canopy. He was so startled by what he saw that he couldn't stop laughing. He laughed and laughed all the way home.

Of course, his brothers wanted to know what he was laughing about, and he told them. "That red bud tree has the most ridiculous name. There were no red buds—just black beans hanging down from the branches. It should be called the Bean Tree."

"No, no you're wrong!" said the eldest brother. "It was so desolate, with just a bare trunk and bare branches, it should be called the Dead Tree."

"Wait a minute," said the third brother. "It had leaves—they looked just like spinach. Yuck! It should be called the Dread Tree."

"Are you all blind?" asked the second brother. "How could you have missed seeing that beautiful tree? The magenta blossoms are like the sunrise. That whole tree was ablaze with them. It is truly a magnificent red bud tree."

The young princes fell into a fierce argument, each prince as adamant as the others that he—and only he—knew the truth.

"I'm right!"

"Don't be ridiculous, I'm right!"

"No, no, no I'm right!"

The king and the chariot driver smiled to themselves. They knew. And you do too that each of them had seen the red bud tree, but in a different season.

Now, if only those princes would stop and listen. If only they'd stop and think. Then they would agree that they had all seen the red bud tree. They might even agree that it truly is magnificent in all the seasons, each in its own way.

FOR REFLECTION

- Why might the princes have been reluctant to share their experiences?
- Can you think of a time when you have kept an experience to yourself that might have been easier to understand, or that you might have understood more deeply, had you talked about it?
- When have you discovered that you saw only one side of a story? What helped you make that discovery?
- What might the tree represent? What in your life has "changed with the seasons"?

THEMES

arrogance, assumptions, awe, beauty, belief, change, conflict, discernment, diversity, doubt, imagination, individualism, interdependence, limitations, mystery, nature, revelation, searching, truth, wholeness, wonder

PRINCIPLES

- Acceptance of one another and encouragement to spiritual growth
- Free and responsible search for truth and meaning

- Four princes hear stories about a magnificent red bud tree and want to see it.
- Late in the winter, the eldest prince has an opportunity.
- He is alone in the chariot with the driver. The driver reluctantly agrees to take him to the tree, and they follow a long, windy road. The prince sees that one tree is different from all the others.
- The eldest prince is disappointed. He returns home feeling sad but says nothing.
- A few months later the second prince has the same opportunity.
- The second prince is awed. He returns home full of joy but says nothing.
- Later, the third prince convinces the driver to take him to the tree.
- The third prince is unpleasantly surprised. He returns home feeling bitter but says nothing.
- Later, the fourth prince is taken to the tree.
- The prince is startled and can't stop laughing.
- He is still laughing when he arrives at home. He reveals having seen the tree but says it's a bean tree not a red bud tree.
- The brothers argue. The first calls it a dead tree; the third calls it a dread tree; the second says it is a red bud tree.
- The king knows, as do you: It is the same tree in different seasons.
- If only the princes would talk! If only they'd listen, then they would know too!

Crow and Pitcher

▣ ▪ ▣ ▪ ▣

This classic Aesop's fable, featuring a clever crow, honors thinking outside the box and reminds us that small acts can have big results.

IT WAS A HOT SUMMER DAY. Crow thought he might die of thirst if he didn't find water soon.

On wilted wings, he allowed himself to be carried hither and thither by the thermal winds. He rode them lazily until, suddenly, something caught his eye.

It was a pitcher perched on a garden table far below. The crow circled down to rest for a moment on its rim. He then bent down and poked his bill inside it. He couldn't reach the water. The pitcher was half empty, and his bill was not long enough.

The crow felt thirstier than ever, with water so close and yet out of reach. He teetered on the edge of the pitcher, feeling full of gloom.

But as he looked around the garden, an idea came to him. He sprang into action. Crow had noticed a pile of pebbles beneath the garden table. He flew down and picked up a "bill-full." He dropped the pebbles into the water, then flew down to collect some more. He repeated this several times over.

With each "bill-full" of pebbles, the water rose just a little higher in the pitcher.

After many trips, the water nearly reached the top.

Crow bent down, drank his fill, and smiled a very satisfied smile.

EXTENSION   You may wish to use this story to honor someone in your community who has been innovative in problem solving or instrumental in coordinating a project. For example, here's a possible extension to the story that might inspire you to find your own variation.

I'd never thought of Al as a crow, but I'm beginning to think he must be at least part corvid. Here is how I see it:

With a layout editor but no content editor, the newsletter pitcher was half empty. Things were looking bleak. Everyone loved their publication and wanted it to continue, but how could it without a full staff? Some searched high, some searched low, and Dorothy searched all around, but for quite a while, it seemed that the newsletter was going to become a fond memory.

Suddenly, Al swooped down. In his view, the pitcher was half-full. He knew that all it needed were a bunch of pebbles. He "threw some in" with his offer to take on the job of content editor, and the possibility of a newsletter bubbled higher. But Al is no ordinary corvid—he likes to share. And so he invited jackdaws, jays, ravens, and even wrens, geese, and parrots like us to throw in what they had in the way of newsworthy tidbits. Each of them was happy to find a small handful of pebbles and equally happy that they didn't have to contribute more than that. Now the newsletter "pitcher" is almost overflowing and we are able to smile again as we drink our fill of news, views, and inspirations.

By the way, anyone else who has some pebbles for the next newsletter is more than welcome to toss them Al's way.

FOR REFLECTION

- When have small acts made a big difference in your life?
- When has thinking outside the box helped you?
- What are some things that encourage you to think more creatively?
- When has working with others made a difference?

THEMES

community, creativity, despair, discernment, failure, hope, imagination, intuition, leadership, patience, service, success, teamwork, unity, vision, weakness, work, worry

PRINCIPLES

- Acceptance of one another and encouragement to spiritual growth
- Right of conscience and use of the democratic process
- Respect for the interdependent web of existence

STORY MAP

- It is a hot day and crow is dying of thirst.
- He sees a pitcher of water on a table.
- He can't reach the water inside.
- Crow is despondent for a moment but then notices some pebbles.
- He flies down to gather some.
- He adds the pebbles one by one to the pitcher and the water rises.
- He can now reach the water and drink his fill.

One Thousand Ideas, One Idea

◨ ▪ ◨ ▪ ◨

Often we fall into the trap of thinking that more is better, not only in terms of material objects but also in terms of ideas. This Russian folktale suggests that focusing with clarity on a single plan can have a better result than trifling with thousands of ideas.

A PEASANT FARMER DECIDED to set a trap in order to capture an animal. He dug a large hole along the path and covered it over with sticks and leaves.

In the middle of the night, a fox trotted along the path and stepped on the sticks covering the hole. He fell straight down into it and was frantic.

The fox paced back and forth and talked to himself as he strategized an escape plan. "I've got an idea! Here's another idea! Oh, or maybe I could do this?" So it went for a while until it was almost dawn, and he was interrupted.

A crane who had been gracefully striding along the path had also stepped on the trap and, with a crash and a thump, had also fallen into the hole.

Naturally, the crane was unhappy! But she was glad to be taller than the fox and to have a very long bill. She moved into one corner of the hole and began to peck the ground.

The fox resumed his frantic pacing. Back and forth, forth and back he went. By now he was bragging, "I've got thousands of ideas! Thousands!"

[*You might want to interject now and then to ask your audience what his ideas might be.*]

The crane stared for a moment, then said, "I've got only one idea." She resumed pecking the ground.

Now it was the fox's turn to stare. He thought, "What a stupid crane. Only one idea! Does she think she can dig her way out of trouble by pecking and pecking at the ground? How ridiculous!"

The sun rose higher in the sky. The animals heard the peasant return to the trap. Before he had removed the brush from above them, the fox began to race faster and faster all around the hole. The crane barely moved. Her body slumped down into the hole she had dug. Her head was twisted to one side of her body, and her legs stretched stiffly into the air. She looked as though she had died of fright.

When the peasant was able to see down into the hole, he roared, "You nasty fox! You've been eating my bird!"

He grabbed the crane's legs and pulled her out of the hole, scolding the fox all the more when he realized the bird was still warm.

The fox continued racing about, not sure which of his thousand ideas to put into action.

While the peasant busied himself with trying to capture the fox, the crane stood up on her very long legs. She implemented her one idea by spreading her wings and flying off to safety.

The fox and his thousands of ideas met an outcome that was far less happy—at least for him.

On the other hand, the peasant was pleased to now have a much warmer collar on his coat.

FOR REFLECTION

- When has having a lot of ideas been helpful to you? When has it been a hindrance?
- What are some of your strategies for coping when you feel trapped?
- When have you experienced the benefits of focus?
- What might cause us to assume that another person's actions make no sense, when it fact they do?

THEMES

activism, anti-oppression, arrogance, assumptions, choice, commitment, conflict, creativity, discernment, faith, fear, hope, humility, imagination, intuition, leadership, limitations, mindfulness, patience, respect, self-care, self-respect, simplicity, solidarity, strength, teamwork, trust, vision, vulnerability, weakness, work, worry, worth

PRINCIPLES

- Inherent worth and dignity of every person
- Acceptance of one another and encouragement to spiritual growth
- Free and responsible search for truth and meaning
- Respect for the interdependent web of all existence

STORY MAP

- A peasant sets a trap by digging a hole in the road and covering it.
- A fox gets trapped. It begins pacing frantically.
- The fox comes up with thousands of escape ideas.
- A crane gets trapped. It assesses its safety trapped with the fox and moves to a corner.
- The crane begins to peck a hole there.
- The fox continues pacing and repeats, "I've got a thousand ideas!"
- The crane says, "I've got one idea."
- The fox thinks the crane is stupid and assumes that the crane is trying to dig its way out of the hole.
- The peasant returns to the trap. The fox paces still more quickly. The crane slumps over and freezes.
- The peasant assumes the fox has killed the crane and is angry.
- The peasant pulls the crane out and becomes even more angry.
- The peasant gets busy capturing the fox.
- The crane implements its one idea and flies off.
- The fox is made into a fur collar.

177

The Monkey Who Asked for Misery

This humorous story from Haiti underscores the importance of not jumping to conclusions. It also cautions us to think carefully about what we ask for. Its optimistic ending is a relief!

MONKEY SAT WAY UP HIGH in the branches of a tree. From there, he had a good overview of everything that was going on. He could see the nearby fields, the forest, and the path that connected them.

As he sat there, a woman came along, carrying a calabash on her head. She was singing:

> I'm on my way to the market place,
> sweet cane syrup in my calabash.
> I'll see my friends. I'll sell my wares.
> I'm gonna come home with plenty o' cash.

She sang it a second time.

> I'm on my way to the market place,
> Sweet cane syrup in my calabash.
> I'll see my friends. I'll sell my wares.
> I'm gonna come home with plenty o'. . . .

"Oh misery!" she yowled.

"Oh misery, misery, misery," she howled. A root at the foot of Monkey's tree had tripped her. Her calabash had slipped off her head and fallen to the ground. It had broken into a thousand pieces. The syrup was oozing out in all directions.

"Papa God," she shouted, "Why do you give me so much misery?" Then she turned on her heels and ran on home.

"Misery, what's that?" wondered Monkey. There was only one way to find out! Monkey swung from one branch of the tree to another, all the way down to the ground.

He cautiously dipped a finger into the sticky liquid. He cautiously put that finger into his mouth. "Mmmh," thought Monkey, "This misery sure is sweet."

He took another cautious finger-full to be sure. It was still sweet. He took another finger-full and another finger-full. Pretty soon he was using his whole hand—then both of them. He kept slurping until every last drop of misery was gone. He wished there was more!

He reached back up to the lowest branch of the tree, then swung himself from branch to branch all the way to the top of the tree.

There, at the top of the tree, he called out, "Papa God, Papa God, please may I have some more misery?"

That was enough to wake Papa God. "Misery? Are you sure you want misery?"

"Oh yes," answered Monkey. "I am very fond of misery!"

"Are you really, really, really certain it's misery you want?"

"Of course!"

"Well," said Papa God. "I can certainly give you some misery if that is what you want."

179

"It's what I want," insisted Monkey. "It's what I want more than anything in the world. Lots and lots of misery."

Papa God bustled about, getting things ready. "Here is a big sack of misery especially for you, Monkey."

"Thank you! Thank you!" Monkey was bursting with excitement.

Before Papa God let go of the sack, he said, "You must not open it until you get to a place where there are no trees. Where there isn't even a single tree."

"No trees?"

"No trees."

Monkey put that sack of misery on his back and began to swing from one tree to another. He kept swinging until he came to the very last tree at the edge of the forest. He adjusted the sack on his back, and then he started walking.

He walked and walked and kept walking until finally he couldn't see a single tree. He put the sack down on the ground.

He was so excited that he could hardly undo the knot. He pulled at it and he poked at it until finally the sack was open!

It wasn't sweet cane syrup that came pouring out of that sack. It was two dogs! They began chasing Monkey, running and jumping and barking. Monkey ran as fast as he could, but those dogs were right behind him. They nipped at his heels!

Monkey ran and ran. He kept on running. He was puffing and panting. His heart was pounding. He didn't think he could get away from those dogs!

And then, all of the sudden, there was a tree.

A tree! Monkey grabbed hold of the lowest branch. He swung himself up, higher and higher. Those dogs ran in circles around the base of that tree.

Monkey heard Papa God laughing and laughing, He called out, "Papa God, why?"

"Oh Monkey, don't you know you've got to be careful what you ask for! Nobody deserves that much misery!"

Monkey scratched his head. As he made his way back to the tree, he thought he heard someone singing.

We live our lives, we make mistakes.

We sometimes get a lucky break.

Things make us glad, or they make us sad.

But we're alive and it's not so bad! [*Repeat*]

NOTE   The refrain is sung to the tune of "Jamaica Farewell" on Harry Belafonte's album *Calypso*. The story can be extended by inviting listeners to learn the song, or shortened by telling the story without the song.

FOR REFLECTION

- What are the kinds of things that seem sweet at first but eventually cause suffering?
- What is it like to have "too much of a good thing"?
- When have you caught yourself or others wanting to be miserable?

THEMES

assumptions, belief, choice, discernment, God/Goddess, greed, happiness, imagination, intuition, limitations, playfulness, reason, searching, success, suffering, truth, wealth

PRINCIPLES

- Acceptance of one another and encouragement to spiritual growth
- Free and responsible search for truth and meaning

STORY MAP

- Monkey sits in the tree tops.
- He sees a woman walking with a calabash full of syrup.
- The woman trips and calls out "Misery!" as she smashes the calabash and the syrup pours out.
- Monkey is curious and tastes the syrup. He says he likes the misery.
- Monkey asks Papa God for more misery. Papa God questions him.

- Papa God gives Monkey a sack of "misery" and tells him to walk until he is far away from all trees.
- Monkey walks far away to a place without trees.
- He opens the sack and two snarling, biting dogs chase him.
- He runs and finally comes to a tree and climbs up it to safety.
- Papa God says to monkey, "Nobody deserves that much misery! Don't you know you've got to be careful what you ask for?"

Accepting Change

The Shining Jewel

⚏ ⚏ ⚏

It is difficult to accept change. It can also be hard to recognize our own gifts. This story is a gentle version of one told by the Skolt Sámi of northern Finland. Only after an extreme situation does an elder begin to understand why younger people in his community question a harsh tradition.

PETSAMO BAY LIES IN THE FAR NORTH where Finland and Norway meet Russia. It has been home to the Skolt Sámi people for a very long time.

In the summer, if you were to walk along the shoreline of the bay, you'd see children hopping from one glistening rock to the next. The sun shines day and night and life is full of joy.

If you stayed until autumn, you'd notice frost wrinkling the earth. As the dark of winter sets in, you'd hear birch leaves crunching underfoot until finally snow blanketed all the earth.

By tradition, when the old people are covered in wrinkles and the chill won't leave their bones, it is time for them to move on to the next life. They find a ways and means to end their lives.

At the time of this story, the old people still insisted on following this harsh tradition. But life had become a little easier at Petsamo Bay, and the young people no longer cared about some of the laws of their people.

So it was for Alexei, whose father Ontri was old and wrinkled. Ontri's back hurt, his hips were sore, his knees cracked. Eating no longer gave him pleasure. Cloudberries and smoked caribou had lost their flavor. Many of his peers were gone, and their absence reminded him of Skolt traditions. He told his family that his time had come.

"No father, not you! I will care for you in your old age."

But Ontri was determined. He had followed Skolt Sámi tradition all his life and knew what was demanded now. His voice cracked, "I know, and you know, and all our neighbors know that it is my time to go."

Alexei bent down as if to kiss his father goodbye. Instead, he picked the old man up and began to walk.

As he carried his father out the door of that cottage and along the shore, he said, "You insist on taking your life into your hands, but I insist on helping you."

Though the old man struggled and pounded him, Alexei continued until they arrived at a small grotto. He lay his father on a bench that stood along the wall. Then he raced home to fetch a proper bedroll, a blanket, his father's birch burl mug, and a sack filled with flatbread and dried berries, fish, and meat.

"I will care for you here." said Alexei. "The neighbors will never know."

Ontri scowled, but before long, he began to chew on a piece of caribou jerky. He *was* a little hungry.

The cave was nestled inside the cliffs that rose up from Petsamo Bay. The moist air and the rhythmic lapping of waves comforted Ontri as he lay on his bedroll. He was sure death would come to him soon.

But the fact was that Ontri was healthy for a man of his age. As the days dragged on, he remained alive and alert. To his surprise, he felt a pang of envy when he heard the young men fishing in the rich waters near the cave.

A day or two later, a fierce storm struck the shores of Petsamo Bay. Ontri could hear the wind howl and branches lash the air. He shuddered as the rain pounded down and waves pummeled against the cliff. Suddenly there was a loud roar and a crash. It sounded as though a big section of cliff had broken off not far from the grotto. He listened as it tumbled into the water.

In the quiet that followed the storm, Ontri heard a young man return to the shore. He peeked out. The young man was gazing into the water. And then the young man peeled off his clothes and dived into the icy depths. What was he after?

Carefully and quietly, Ontri stepped out of the cave. Across from him, he could see something glistening on the fresh scar of the landslide.

He waited for the young man to return. But the cold water had been too much to bear. The young man was gone.

Ontri watched more men arrive. All became mesmerized by the shimmering in the sea. One man after another began to remove his clothes. They were preparing to dive into the icy water to retrieve the treasure they'd seen.

Ontri scrambled across the rocks as quickly as he could, waving his arms and shouting, "Stop! Stop! Look up! Don't be fools! The jewel in the water is only a reflection."

Alexei heard him first and stopped. He looked up to where his father pointed. There, in the face of the cliff, was a gigantic glistening jewel. It had been exposed when part of the cliff slid into the sea. His father was right—what the young men were after was only a reflection.

He rushed to his father and opened his arms to hug him. Ontri felt his heart grow warm—almost as though he had a shining jewel within. He smiled all the way home and accepted Alexei's invitation to take the warmest bench by the fire.

As they sat together, Ontri mumbled, "Perhaps the old tradition could change."

[You might invite listeners to place their hands on their hearts, to sense the shining jewel inside themselves.]

NOTE   You can hear an example of a leu'dd at http://tinyurl.com/jb50p6c. Perhaps you'll be inspired to include a small chant in your retelling of the story.

FOR REFLECTION

- What are some gifts that an elder has given you?
- What experiences help you feel confident that you have wisdom to share?
- When have you misunderstood where the "true jewel" resides?
- What are some traditions you would like to change? What are some traditions you are reluctant to change?

THEMES

acceptance, aging, beauty, belief, belonging, caring, change, choice, community, culture, death, depression, despair, dignity, discernment, dissent, family, freedom, happiness, identity, illness, inclusion, interdependence, intuition, kindness, limitations, love, loyalty, mystery, parents, pride, purpose, relationships, respect, responsibility, revelation, self-acceptance, self-respect shame, success, suffering, tradition, trust, truth, weakness, worry, worth, youth

PRINCIPLES

- Inherent worth and dignity of every person
- Justice, equity, and compassion in human relations
- Acceptance of one another and encouragement to spiritual growth
- Free and responsible search for truth and meaning
- World community with peace, liberty, and justice for all
- Respect for the interdependent web of all existence

- The Skolt Sámi live at Petsamo Bay in Finland.
- In summer, life with the sun is full of joy. In autumn, frost wrinkles the earth. In winter, the cold is a challenge.
- Skolt Sámi tradition dictates that when elders enter their "autumn," it is time to move on to the next life.
- The elders want to follow tradition, but the younger generation is less keen.
- In one family, the father, Ontri, insists he must "go." The son (Alexei) insists he will care for him.
- Alexei carries his father to a cave where he will care for him. He brings provisions.
- Ontri can't resist eating the caribou jerky. He is not unhealthy. In fact, he feels a little envious when he hears the young men fishing.
- A storm hits. The cliff face slumps into the sea.
- Next day, he hears a young man, peeks out, then watches as the man dives into the water.
- He steps out of the cave and sees something glistening on the newly exposed cliff face.
- He waits, but the young man doesn't return. He has been taken by the cold sea.
- More young men arrive and see something shimmering in the water. They prepare to dive in.
- Ontri yells, "Stop! Look up! The jewel you seek is on the cliff!"
- His son is the first to hear. He realizes that the shimmering in the water is only a reflection.
- He thanks his father.
- Ontri now recognizes that he can still contribute to his family and agrees to return home.

Grandfather and Grandson

⠿ ⠿ ⠿

This is the story that set me on the quest to relate wisdom tales to my life. Another teller said I was living this story when I told her about my decision to bring my children to visit their grandparents instead of going on a "real" holiday. It's been retold many times by storytellers around the world. Similar tales are found in Korea, Ireland, and Latin America.

HE WAS OLD. His wife had died. His son and daughter-in-law invited him to move in with them.

In the few years that he had lived there, he'd grown more and more frail, more forgetful and clumsy.

It was hard for the daughter-in-law. She had so much to see to already, with the children, the garden, and thc household chores.

One day, it was suddenly too much. He'd knocked over his bowl yet again. Not only had the soup spilled all over the table and soiled the beautiful embroidered cloth but the old man had broken yet another one of her few fine bowls.

That night when the grandfather sat outside, the daughter-in-law said to her husband, "You must carve or buy a wooden bowl for the old man."

"A wooden bowl?"

"I'm tired of him breaking my good dishes. Better he eat from something that won't be ruined if he drops it."

Having broached the subject of her father-in-law, it was as though a dam had burst. Her many grievances poured forth.

"I'm tired of the way he complains. He'll say the tea is cold, but that's because he forgets to drink it. I'm tired of the way he changes his mind. He doesn't ever seem to know what to do. I'm tired of his endless chatter. He says the same things over and again."

She went on, "It's embarrassing when neighbors come by. Perhaps we can set a table for him in the nook around the corner."

The man understood his wife's complaints. He too found it challenging to live with his father. He may have been about to suggest a solution even more drastic. We'll never know.

A sudden movement caught his eye, and his wife's.

It was their son. He was rummaging about, looking for something.

"What are you up to, Sweetie?" asked the mother.

"Oh, just looking for some wood."

"What for?"

[You might ask your audience if they know.]

"I'm going to start carving wooden bowls for you and dad. I want to be all ready for when you get old."

The boy's parents stared at the boy, and then at one another. At that moment, they understood how wrong they had been. The father went outside to invite the grandfather to join them for tea. The daughter-in-law set the grandfather's favorite cup and saucer before him. They were made of porcelain.

There was no more talk of a wooden bowl, nor of a nook around the corner.

FOR REFLECTION

- When have you noticed an elder being treated as less worthy?
- When has someone younger than you offered a fresh perspective?

THEMES

acceptance, aging, anger, arrogance, belonging, caring, change, children, choice, compassion, conflict, conscience, dignity, dissent, empathy, equality, family, generosity, kindness, limitations, parents, patience, reason, relationships, respect, rights, shame, vulnerability, weakness, wholeness, worth, youth

PRINCIPLES

- Inherent worth and dignity of every person
- Justice, equity, and compassion in human relations
- Acceptance of one another and encouragement to spiritual growth
- World community with peace, liberty, and justice for all
- Respect for the interdependent web of all existence

STORY MAP

- Grandfather is old and has moved in with his son and daughter-in-law.
- While there, he becomes less capable and more of a challenge for his busy daughter-in-law.
- One day, Grandfather knocks over the soup bowl "again."
- The bowl breaks; the soup spills and stains the table cloth. This is too much for the daughter-in-law.
- That evening, the daughter-in-law tells her husband that they need a wooden bowl for the old man.
- She shares many other grievances about her father-in-law. The husband is understanding and in agreement.
- Suddenly the man notices his son and asks what he is doing.
- The boy is looking for wood. He wants to carve wooden bowls in preparation for their old age.
- The husband and wife regret their behavior.
- They show compassion for the old man and drop all talk of giving him a wooden bowl.

Donald of the Burdens

⚃ ⚃ ⚃

All around the world, as a way of coping with the inevita-
bility of death, people tell humorous stories about it. This
tale from Scotland could also be a springboard to think more
purposefully about some of the choices we make in life and
to consider whether there ever is an easy way out. An almost
identical tale to this one is found in Mexico.

IN SCOTLAND, they tell the story of a man called Donald of the
Burdens whose job was to keep the laird's manor supplied with
wood.

It was no easy feat. There were many fireplaces in that grand
home and much wood was needed to keep them burning. And so
Donald's back was forever bent with the burden of a huge stack
of wood.

One day, when he was crossing from the forest toward the
manor house, a stranger stopped and asked, "Would you like
another job?"

Donald looked up.

"Would you like to be a doctor?" inquired the man.

"A doctor? Me?" laughed Donald. "How could someone like
me ever become a doctor?"

"I'll help you," answered the man. "It won't be difficult. With me, you'll always be able to make an honest diagnosis."

Donald looked at the stranger quizzically.

"I am Death," said the man. "And whenever you visit a patient, I'll be right there, but visible to your eyes only."

"If I'm at the foot of the bed, it means the patient will get better. Prescribe something. Anything. Perhaps a little chamomile tea and some rest. Whatever you give them, the patient will recover."

"On the other hand, if I'm standing at the head of the bed, you'll know that the patient's time has come. You can offer comfort and solace, but don't bother trying a cure. It won't be possible."

"Is it truly as simple as that?"

"It is," replied Death. "But do not cheat me! If you try to trick me in any way, you will be mine!"

Donald could not wait to set down his burdens. He accepted the offer.

Soon enough, he had earned himself a good reputation as a doctor, and was earning a good living too. People knew they could count on his diagnoses. The cures he prescribed always worked.

Donald became so well renowned as a fine physician that when the king fell ill, he was summoned.

He entered the king's chamber and immediately saw Death standing by the king's head. He bowed low and began to offer solace to all in the room.

The queen refused to accept Donald's swift diagnosis. "But this is the king! Surely you can do something!"

When she saw Donald hesitate, she continued, "I am the queen. You are my servant! I command you to do whatever is in your power to cure the king." She stared at Donald unwaveringly.

Donald flinched. How could he disobey the queen? He knew there was one way that he could help the king recover. He motioned to a guard and gave discreet instructions about a plan to administer the cure.

Donald and the guard took positions at either end of the bed. They bent over the king and swiftly lifted and turned him around in the bed. Now the king's head was at the other end of the bed and Death was by his feet!

For a moment, Death stared at Donald in outrage. He was not about to let go of his prize. He hurried to the other end of the bed to sit by the king's head once more.

What do you suppose Donald did?

He motioned to the guard. The two men bent over the king once more and swiftly lifted and turned him around in the bed. Now his head was at the other end of the bed and Death was by his feet again.

[*You might involve your audience in the following sequence.*]

What do you suppose Death did?

He hurried to sit beside the king's head once more!

What do you suppose Donald did?

He and the guard turned the king once more!

And so it went, back and forth, forth and back. Donald of the Burdens was a strong and energetic man. So was the guard. They moved the king so many times that, finally, Death gave up. He left the palace in a rage.

A calm fell over the king's chamber. For the first time since he'd been summoned, all in the room felt a gentle breeze drifting in through the window, carrying birdsong and the sweet aroma of spring flowers.

A few moments later, the king opened his eyes. Everyone rejoiced! The guards, the servants, the ladies-in-waiting, and the butler thanked Donald. The queen nodded her head, and even the king smiled in appreciation.

A huge sack of gold was pressed into Donald's arms. Soon enough, he was on his way home.

He hadn't gone far down the forest trail, when who do you suppose emerged from the woods?

It was Death himself. He took Donald firmly by the hand and what do you suppose he said?

"You were dishonest. You broke your promise. You tricked me out of my prize and now you are mine."

Death lead Donald away, and Donald of the Burdens was no more.

———

FOR REFLECTION

- How does a story like this help us deal with death?
- When do you think Donald's burden is heaviest?
- What are some current ways we "trick" death or the aging process?

THEMES

acceptance, aging, choice, class, compassion, covenant, creativity, death, dissent, failure, grief, illness, letting go, limitations, power, purpose, regret, service, success, suffering, truth, vulnerability, weakness, work

PRINCIPLE

- Free and responsible search for truth and meaning

STORY MAP

- In Scotland, Donald has the back-breaking job of supplying the manor house with wood.
- One day, a stranger offers him a job as a doctor. Donald feels he doesn't qualify.
- The stranger explains that he is Death. With his help, Donald will diagnose correctly.
- When Death is at the foot of the bed, the patient will recover. When Death is at the head of the bed, the patient will die.
- Death warns Donald not to cheat. If he does, Death will take him.
- Donald accepts the job and soon earns a good reputation.

- The king falls ill and the queen summons "Doctor" Donald.
- Donald sees Death at the head of the bed and says a cure is impossible.
- The queens begs and then insists that he try.
- Donald considers. He asks a guard for help and whispers the instructions.
- Donald and the guard swiftly turn the king so that Death is at his feet.
- Death is angry but hurries to sit beside the king's head.
- Donald and the guard repeat the "cure" several times. Death moves several times.
- Finally Death gives up and leaves the palace in a rage.
- The king recovers. Donald is richly rewarded.
- Donald leaves the palace.
- Death is waiting for him in the woods. "Death always gets his prize."

Capturing
Spring

Stories of fools can be found in many cultures. The written form of The Wise Men of Gotham *dates back to thirteenth-century England. While all the tales in the collection portray fools, they were woven with the purpose of persuading King John that the people of Gotham were mad. This was to discourage the king's entourage from passing through the village and burdening the residents with heavy taxes—not so foolish after all! This story emphasizes the impossibility of trying to control nature and the necessity of accepting the inevitable. It might be told at a celebration of spring, or when it's time to remember humility.*

IT WAS DEEP WINTER, and just like the rest of us, the men of Gotham looked forward to thc turning of the year.

"Spring time," ruminated one. "What could be better? I love the greening of the leaves and the singing of the birds. Everything is so hopeful and happy."

"If only," mused another, "It could be spring all year!"

As they chewed on that wish, one and then another had a question to ask.

"What is it that heralds the spring?" The others replied in unison, "the cuckoo!"

"What is it that wakes the sun?" The others replied in unison, "the cuckoo!" [*You might pause so that your audience has time to answer too.*]

"What is it that urges the leaves to unfurl and the flowers to bloom?" The others replied in unison, "the cuckoo!" [*By now, your audience will answer with you.*]

Almost in unison, the fools of Gotham exclaimed, "If only we could trap the cuckoo, we could have spring all year."

They knew that the cuckoo loved to hide in thick bush. And so they planned and planted and pruned until they had the perfect circle of bush, round as a compass, with the branches stretched up like the bars on a birdcage.

Come spring, it wasn't hard to lure a cuckoo inside that birdcage bush. Once there, the men of Gotham promised the bird, "Sing here all year and you'll never lack food or drink."

With these words, the cuckoo realized they were trying to cage her. She, who'd once been so happy to sing for them, would sing for them no more! She, who they thought was caged, could see an escape route overhead. She cried out, [*with a gesture, here and at the end, you can probably get your audience to sing out, "Cuckoo!"*] "Cuckoo! You're cuckoo!" and off she flew.

The fools of Gotham lamented, "If only we'd made the walls higher."

I imagine that the response they heard was, "Cuckoo! You're cuckoo!"

FOR REFLECTION

- What might "spring" represent? What are some of the things we do to "capture" spring?
- When have you experienced a "solution" that wasn't thought through fully?
- When have you noticed an attempt to control something that can't be controlled?

THEMES

acceptance, arrogance, assumptions, beauty, belief, change, discernment, Earth, environment, failure, greed, happiness, joy, letting go, limitations, nature, patience, reason, stewardship, teamwork, trust, vision, wonder

PRINCIPLES

- Free and responsible search for truth and meaning
- Respect for the interdependent web of all existence

STORY MAP

- In deep winter, the "wise men" of Gotham look forward to spring.
- They wish spring would last all year long.
- They figure that if they capture the cuckoo, so that it is there to herald spring all year, spring will also last all year.
- They know that the cuckoo hides in the bush, and so they work together to create a perfect circular cage out of the bush.
- In the spring, they lure the cuckoo into the bush cage.
- At first, the cuckoo refuses to sing. Then the cuckoo flies off via the escape route he sees overhead.
- The wise men lament, "if only we'd made the cage taller."

A Pig's Life

No matter how wise we are, we can't truly understand what
the future will be like. This story, from Andhra Pradesh in
southern India, pokes fun at certainty. It also emphasizes
that all forms of life are as worthy and valuable as our own.

ONCE THERE WAS A GURU who had meditated for so long that
he had developed the gift of seeing into the future.

People from miles around flocked to see him. They all wanted
to know what was in store for them. But the guru felt uneasy
about sharing too much; instead he would only say, "Have faith,
live a good life!"

To be honest, he felt that knowing the future only made life
more difficult. In fact, his knowledge about what lay ahead for
him made it challenging to have faith at times. The problem was
that he knew that his destiny was to become a pig in his next life.

A pig?

The guru had tried to live a good and pure life; it puzzled him
to no end why he would have such a strange and lowly destiny. He
thought that perhaps in past lives he had accumulated a great deal
of bad karma that he hadn't yet paid off. For a long time, he
fussed and worried about the situation. Then remembering that
he was a guru, he went back to meditation.

One day after a particularly long and deep session, he suddenly arrived at a perfect solution. He called for his most loyal

disciple and, to be certain, asked "Will you do anything I ask?" The man replied, "I am your disciple, I know that all you ask will be for the good. Of course I will do it."

"Thank you," said the guru. He cleared his throat a little and added, "First, you must know that I am destined to be a pig in my next life."

The disciple's jaw dropped.

The guru was quick to explain that he was certain it must have to do with his past lives. "But, you can help me."

"Please, after I die, watch for my birth. As a pig, I will have the same birthmark on my forehead that I have now." The disciple nodded.

"Good, good. When you see me, you must kill me straight away."

The disciple was aghast—he had never harmed anything. He wasn't sure he could do such a thing.

But the guru reassured him. He explained his perfect plan, "Pigs are unclean—it is no sin to kill them. And the sooner I die as a pig, the sooner I will move on to my next life, on a higher plane."

The disciple trusted his guru. He shook away his hesitance and nodded in agreement. Yes, he could and would do as his guru had asked.

Not long afterward, the guru became ill and died.

After the funeral, the disciple visited the neighboring farms every day. The barns were dirty and smelly. He pinched his nose and bravely avoided the "mud pies" so that he could check on the animals in their pens.

Within a few weeks, one of the sows gave birth to twenty-one piglets. Sure enough, on close inspection, the disciple saw that one of them had a birthmark on its forehead just like the guru's mark.

The disciple reached hesitantly for the knife he had hidden in the folds of his robe. It was there.

With some difficulty, he grabbed the squirming piglet. He held the fleshy animal close to his chest. It wriggled, trying to escape, but the disciple hung on tightly. He grimaced as he summoned the courage to bring the knife blade to the piglet's throat. But before he did, he heard a high-pitched squeak. It almost sounded like words were coming out of the piglet's mouth!

The disciple listened more closely. Sure enough, the piglet was speaking. It was saying, "Stop, don't kill me! As my loyal disciple, I command you not to kill me."

The disciple was shocked! Should he obey the words of the piglet? Or should he obey the words of the man?

Before he could decide, the piglet continued, "I know that in my past life I told you to kill me, but that was before I knew what it was like to be a pig. The mud is soft and silky. My mother's belly is warm and comforting. Her milk flows freely and tastes as sweet as honey. A pig's life is a good life. I truly believe that it is a fair reward for my past life."

The disciple was more amazed than ever, and more than a little relieved. He set his master down next to the sow's teats. He watched for a moment as the piglet snuggled up with its mother.

As he walked down to the river to wash off the filth from the barn, he shook his head thinking, "How strange it is that you can know the future and yet not understand it at all."

FOR REFLECTION

- When have your assumptions been wrong about what another person's or being's life is like?
- When has something you thought would be a "disaster" proven to be a gift?
- How might "loving the mud" change your life?

THEMES

acceptance, aging, animals, arrogance, assumptions, awe, birth, change, choice, conscience, covenant, death, dignity, discernment, ethics, faith, fear, happiness, hope, humility, identity, imagination, joy, listening, mindfulness, mystery, revelation, self-acceptance, simplicity, transformation, truth, wholeness, worry

PRINCIPLES

- Inherent worth and dignity of every person
- Acceptance of one another and encouragement to spiritual growth
- Free and responsible search for truth and meaning

STORY MAP

- A guru develops the gift of knowing what the future holds.
- Many are envious. The guru finds it a burden.
- For example, he knows that he will become a pig in his next life.
- He is puzzled and thinks it must be a result of his failures in a past life.
- He meditates on it and finds a solution.
- He asks his most faithful disciple to help. The disciple promises that he will do anything.
- The guru reveals that his future is to become a pig and that, as a pig, he will have the same birthmark as the guru.
- He insists the disciple find and kill him when he has become a pig.
- The disciple is horrified, but he trusts his guru so eventually agrees.
- The guru dies.
- The disciple checks local farms. He is uncomfortable with the mess of animals.
- He finds a piglet with the guru's birthmark.
- He picks up the piglet, finds his knife, and prepares to kill the piglet when he thinks he hears the piglet speak.
- The piglet squeals, "Stop, don't kill me!"
- The disciple is uncertain. Should he obey a piglet or his guru?
- The piglet explains, "Life is wonderful as a pig. I hadn't anticipated how good it would be."
- The disciple sets the piglet down.

Seeking Peace and Finding Hope

The Almond Tree

"Paying it forward" is not such a new idea, nor is it ever too late to do what we can to ensure a bright future. Inspired by a tale from the Talmud and a similar one from Turkey, this modern retelling is a perfect way to honor trees and the environment or to celebrate aging.

TALIA'S FACE WAS LIKE a complicated map, full of ridges and wrinkles. Her back was bent over. And when she walked, she shuffled.

Still, she had a twinkle in her eye, and she always had a kind word for her neighbors, her children, her grandchildren, and her great-grandchildren.

She spent most of her days in her rocking chair, looking out over her garden. If she had a visitor, she'd share memories of the good old days. When she was alone, she'd remember to herself. Now and then, she'd hum a little or wiggle her fingers.

It was during one of those mornings alone that Talia surprised herself by coming up with an ambitious decision. She made a phone call. A few hours later, when the doorbell rang, the delivery man was patient while she slowly shuffled her way to the door.

She directed him to carry the very tall skinny parcel he had brought to a bare corner of the garden. He kindly helped her find the garden spade and pull a lawn chair over. Then she paid him and waved him off.

Slowly, very slowly, she dug a big hole in the ground. It was hard work. Now and then she'd sit on the lawn chair to take a break. But she got back up several times until, eventually, the hole was just the right size.

Slowly, very slowly, she shuffled and rotated the bottom of the tall, skinny parcel into the hole. Kerplunk. She sat back down to inspect it and was satisfied.

Slowly, very slowly, she began to push the dirt back into the hole all around the bottom of the parcel. That too was hard work. Over and again, when she got tired, she sat down on the lawn chair to take a break. Then she got back up, and finally she was finished.

She unwrapped that tall skinny parcel. And there it was. You've probably guessed—a beautiful sapling tree! She sat down once again to admire it.

About then, her neighbor arrived home and poked her head over the fence. She looked alarmed and said, "Talia, you be careful! What are you doing? Planting a tree? Ridiculous! Someone your age! Is it an almond tree? It won't produce almonds for years!"

Talia laughed as she pointed at a very old tree in the opposite corner of her garden. Some of its branches were broken right off, others were bent with age. Most of them were bare, even though it was the middle of spring.

She said, "I'm like that old almond tree. My great-grandmother planted it. I loved to climb it when I was a little girl. Its branches were broad and strong. I felt safe there."

"Then, when I was a young woman, I picked some of its delicate pink blossom and decorated my hair with them. I think that's how my husband came to notice me!"

The neighbor began to smile. As usual, there was no stopping Talia or her story.

"When I was a mother, I picked the almonds, roasted them to perfection, and served them to my family. When I was a grandmother, I rested in the shade of the almond tree. Now I am a great-grandmother."

Talia was looking very dreamy as she continued, "I have lots of time on my hands. I sit and remember as I look out my window. Mostly, I am happy with my life. But a little while ago as I sat looking out into my garden, I realized that I had never planted a tree. Never. It just didn't seem right! I have great-grandchildren."

"Great-grandchildren?" asked the neighbor.

Talia exclaimed, "Yes! They need an almond tree."

"Of course!" laughed the neighbor, as she pledged to herself to do something for her great-grandchildren too, even though she didn't yet have any.

I wonder what that will be. Perhaps she will plant a tree.

What do you think?

And as for Talia—after planting the tree, she returned to her rocking chair to look out her window, and smile.

FOR REFLECTION

- What are some of the things you do that take future generations into consideration?
- What makes it difficult to take action that benefits the future?
- How has your appreciation of thinking ahead changed over the years?

THEMES

activism, aging, calling, caring, change, character, children, choice, commitment, community, connection, conscience, contemplation, covenant, death, discernment, environment, faith, family, generosity, gratitude, history, hope, interdependence, leadership, love, mindfulness, nature, parents, patience, purpose, responsibility, service, stewardship, success, vision, work, worth

PRINCIPLES

- Inherent worth and dignity of every person
- Free and responsible search for truth and meaning
- World community with peace, liberty, and justice for all
- Respect for the interdependent web of all existence

STORY MAP

- Talia is an old woman with a twinkle in her eyes.
- She spends her time relaxing and enjoying life.
- One day when she is sitting alone, she makes a big decision.
- She orders a package by phone. A delivery man arrives with a tall narrow parcel.
- He carries it into the garden and helps by bringing Talia a spade and an armchair.
- Very slowly, Talia digs a large hole, taking rests now and then.
- Finally she places the parcel in the hole and fills around it with dirt.
- She unwraps the parcel to reveal an almond sapling. The neighbor thinks Talia is crazy. She thinks this is way too much work and questions Talia.
- Talia points to a very old (dying) tree that her great-grandmother planted.
- She says that as a child, she loved to climb it. As a girl, she decorated her hair with its blossoms. As a mother, she picked and roasted its almonds. As a grandmother, she rested in its shade.
- She is now old but can't rest until she knows that her great-grandchildren will have a tree to enjoy.
- The neighbor is inspired, and Talia is contented.

Cooking Together, Trinidad Style

Stories of making something from nothing appear in folk traditions all around the world. Often they involve making soup from a stone. I've added geographic context and historic detail to this rich variation from Trinidad. In it, a creative woman inspires children and their diverse families to work together.

CALLALOO IS A THICK GREEN SOUP. It's eaten in places like Jamaica and Trinidad where people say that learning to make Callaloo soup is a little like learning to live.

The soup goes way back in time, to the days when the ports of Trinidad were full of tall sailing ships. The local Carib and Arawak people weren't sure what to make of them. Some had sailed from Britain, and others were from France and Spain. The new arrivals included people from China and India, Ghana and Mali. They came from Syria, Portugal, and Venezuela too. Each of the groups arrived on the shores of Trinidad with their own language and songs, their own clothing and food, different from each other and from the people who'd lived on the island forever.

People are people; we're most comfortable with what we know. So even though Trinidad is not a very big place, people stuck closest to their own kind. The Arawaks and Caribs retreated to the forests. The Chinese avoided the French, who avoided the Indians, who mixed as little as possible with the Venezuelans, and so on down the line. Trinidad was a divided nation.

Things might well have stayed that way. But one rainy season, the hurricane trail took a turn toward Trinidad. The storm raged like a beast trampling over the island, tossing and turning everything up.

When the beast finally moved on, all of Trinidad was a terrible mess. Crops were drowned, houses flattened, trees uprooted, and boats smashed to smithereens. The people who survived were scared, and hungry.

You know how it can be when there are shortages—the ugly in us can come out. Sure enough, people grew greedy. It was hard for them to find food, and when they did, they hoarded it for themselves and their own kind. Worry, anger, and jealousy hung over the island like a great black cloud. And the island was more divided than ever.

It might well have stayed that way, but an elderly woman happened to notice something glinting beneath the ruins of a house. What was it? She was curious. She began to pull away the boards and rubble. They were heavy. She had to work hard.

Finally, there it was, a great huge cooking pot. The woman looked at it. "Mmmmh?" she thought. As she began to hatch a plan, a big smile came over her face.

She lit a fire with some of the boards and rubble. She filled her pot with water, added some salt, and began to stir and chant.

"It may be a little bland, but the soup I'm cooking is for every child, woman, and man."

[*You might encourage your audience to join in the above refrain, and interject it between each contribution to the soup.*]

Her chanting was heard far and wide. People grew curious.

"It may be a little bland, but the soup I'm cooking is for every child, woman, and man."

No one wanted soup that was bland! Those who heard hurried home to search through their store of goods.

A Carib family arrived in the square with sweet cocoplums and starchy cocoyams. The woman smiled as they peeled and then plunked them into the pot. An Arawak family followed suit, with fine bud peppers and slices of sweet squash. A family from Mali brought bunches of green okra pods that had survived the storm. A British family delivered salt-pork. An Indian family had found coconuts knocked to the ground; they cracked them open and poured the sweet milk and shavings into the soup. Syrians added cumin, while the Spaniards and French came with garlic, onions, and thyme. A Chinese family contributed the big green leaves of dasheen. They tore the leaves into strips that gave the soup its beautiful deep green color.

Soon the aroma coming from that pot caused people to hum and smile. The smart woman stirred. Her soup was almost finished.

She paused for a few moments, curious about the clamor of children she could hear down at the beach.

A short time later, a big giggling mixed group arrived—they were all colors and shapes and sizes. They'd been too busy helping one another capture crabs to pay attention to cultural differences.

They had buckets full of rich-tasting blue crabs to add to the soup. The smart woman stirred. At last, she announced, "The first ever Callaloo."

The old woman ladled out scoop after scoop of the mysterious mixed-flavor soup into people's bowls and calabashes and cups. It was delicious and hearty! Once their bellies were full, they began to talk and tell stories. They began to sing.

After a while, some of them looked up. They saw that the big black cloud that had been hanging over Trinidad had parted. The skies had opened up and the sun was shining again. The cultural divisions on the Island of Trinidad were breaking down.

It's said that the children who made the first ever Callaloo Soup continued to mix and mingle. It is said that their children were the Callaloo children—children who knew how to get along with people of all cultures, colors, shapes, and sizes.

I say the world needs more Callaloo soup and Callaloo children!

EXTENSION For a festive feel, you may wish to invite listeners to sing the chorus of Jimmy Buffet's song "Callaloo" before, during, and/or after the story.

FOR REFLECTION

- When has a crisis brought out the best in the people around you?
- When have you experienced a situation where people have worked together to create something out of nothing?
- How does having less inspire more creativity? What example from your own life can you think of?
- When has one person in your life made a difference?

THEMES

acceptance, activism, anti-oppression, belonging, calling, change, children, community, covenant, creativity, culture, despair, diversity, fear, generosity, greed, hope, hospitality, identity, imagination, inclusion, interdependence, leadership, multiculturalism, race/ethnicity, reconciliation, relationships, respect, responsibility, service, solidarity, teamwork, transformation, trust, unity, vision, worry

PRINCIPLES

- Inherent worth and dignity of every person
- Justice, equity, and compassion in human relations
- Right of conscience and use of the democratic process
- World community with peace, liberty, and justice for all
- Respect for the interdependent web of all existence

STORY MAP

- Callaloo is a thick green soup served in the Caribbean.
- Some say that learning to make it is like learning to live.
- It developed when strangers from Europe, Africa, Asia, and South America joined the Carib and Arawak people living on Trinidad.
- At first, each cultural group lives separate from the others.
- There is a huge storm that drowns crops, destroys houses, smashes boats, and downs trees.
- People are fearful. Some begin to hoard food and shun others.
- An elderly woman notices a large pot and rescues it from the rubble.
- She pours water and salt into the pot and places it on a fire.
- She claims it is bland soup, but it is for all to share.
- People are intrigued. One after another they retrieve ingredients they had hidden.
- They contribute cocoplums, cocoyams, peppers, squash, okra, garlic, onions, thyme, cumin, coconut, cashews, salt pork, and dasheen.
- With each addition, the woman stirs the pot and smiles.
- Finally, a large flock of children from all different nationalities arrives. They get along despite their different heritages.
- Together they have gathered buckets of blue crabs, which they offer for the soup. The woman stirs the crabs in and is satisfied that the soup is now complete.
- She serves soup to everyone.
- As their bellies fill, people talk and tell stories.
- The black cloud over the island dissipates, as do the cultural divisions.
- The children of those children who helped make the soup are called Callaloo children. They know how to get along with others.

Hannah and the Wind

Where and how do we find the strength to rise above anger and maintain peaceful, neighborly relations? As I envisioned the difficulty of living in the tight quarters depicted in this traditional Jewish story, I added character and setting details and an emphasis on the healing power of nature.

HANNAH FINISHED WASHING her clothing at the village well and carried them back to her home, to hang them on the clothesline. She didn't have a front yard or a back yard, so the clothesline was in the courtyard that she shared with her neighbor.

The clothes began to dance in the wind. Hannah watched for a moment then went inside to prepare the evening meal.

[*You might involve the audience by inviting them to make the sound of the wind whenever it is mentioned in the story. Raise your arms like a conductor to encourage a stronger wind, then lower them until the room magically grows quiet.*]

A few minutes later her neighbor, Sarah, was on her way out the door—off to her vegetable patch to harvest food for supper. She was late and in a hurry. She rushed out and straight into Hannah's clothes that were hanging on the line, right in the middle of her path.

Something snapped inside Sarah. She'd had enough! She grabbed the knife from her basket and cut the clothesline. With great satisfaction, she watched the clothes tumble to the ground and then continued on her way.

Hannah missed all of this. But a little while later, she opened her front door to fetch a few herbs growing in a pot outside. She saw the clothesline and couldn't believe her eyes!

She clenched her fists. She knew at once who it was. She began to walk toward Sarah's door. She was going to pound on it until Sarah answered, and she had a thing or two to say.

But just then, there was a little gust of wind. It seemed to blow in whirls and twirls and whispers. Somehow that caused Hannah to remember what a difficult life Sarah had. She was a single mom, all on her own with three hungry children to feed.

Hannah unclenched her fists. She picked up the clothes, brought them back to the well, rinsed them out, and vigorously wrung out the excess water.

She returned to the courtyard, where she tied the clothesline back together, hung the clothes back up, and then returned to her meal preparations. She hummed a little tune as she chopped vegetables and kneaded the bread dough.

Before long, Hannah's husband arrived home. Usually, Hannah liked to recount the details of the day. But the wind seemed to whistle a little just as he was coming in, and Hannah changed her mind.

Instead, she sat quietly with her husband to enjoy watching the sunset and the gentle movement of the trees in the wind.

Meanwhile, Sarah had a miserable day. She fretted while she worked. Why had she been so rash? Why had she cut the clothesline?

When she returned home, she was happy to see the clothes hanging again, but once she was inside her house, she couldn't stop pacing back and forth, worrying about the unpleasant words she was bound to hear from Hannah. Again and again, she thought she heard Hannah's footsteps outside.

But now it was sunset and still Hannah hadn't come.

"Oh dear," she thought, "I shall have to go and ask forgiveness."

She made her way across the courtyard, carefully moving the clothes aside that still hung on the line. She knocked a little timidly on Hannah's door.

When Hannah opened it, Sarah was most puzzled!

Hannah was not scowling; she did not look worried. In fact, Hannah had a smile on her face.

Sarah apologized profusely.

Hannah took Sarah's hands in her own as she said, "Today I have learned something good. I have learned that the wind doesn't just dry clothes. The wind can sweep away anger."

FOR REFLECTION

- When has letting go of your anger made a difference in your life?
- What helps you let go of anger?
- What are some important steps for creating peace—at home, in local communities, and around the world?

THEMES

anger, blame, brokenness, caring, character, choice, community, compassion, conflict, conscience, contemplation, dignity, discernment, empathy, forgiveness, friendship, generosity, kindness, letting go, nature, peace, reconciliation, regret, relationships, shame, spirituality, transcendence, transformation, vulnerability, work, worry

PRINCIPLES

- Inherent worth and dignity of every person
- Justice, equity, and compassion in human relations
- Acceptance of one another and encouragement to spiritual growth
- World community with peace, liberty, and justice for all

- Hannah hangs her clothes in the courtyard she shares with her neighbor.
- Sarah, her neighbor, finds the clothes in her way as she rushes out of the house. She cuts the clothesline and leaves for work.
- Hannah is outraged.
- The wind dances and whispers to her and reminds Hannah to empathize with Sarah.
- Hannah repairs the clothesline and hangs up her clothes again.
- Hannah's husband returns home and she wants to share the story.
- The wind dances again and reminds Hannah that some stories are best not shared.
- Sarah returns home anticipating Hannah's anger.
- Sarah is surprised when Hannah doesn't come to yell at her.
- Sarah summons the courage to visit Hannah and apologize.
- Hannah welcomes Sarah and Sarah is surprised.
- Hannah explains the gift of the wind.

The Night Bird

Yearning for peace is central to this haunting Russian Roma tale that I've embellished by imagining some of the dialogue that might have taken place. While all of us have a role in creating and maintaining peace, this story stresses both that peacemaking is ultimately a responsibility of leadership and that taking an extreme stance is sometimes necessary. Baro Shero is a taunting Romani term for an ostentatious ruler. I chose to use it as the name of the chief in this story to reflect leadership style.

LONG AGO in the Russian forests and steppe, the Roma people traveled far and wide in separate bands. They camped in the forests and fields, and made their fortunes in the villages they visited.

Life was good when they were on the road and on their own.

Life was good, unless one group of Roma ran into another. Then the chiefs were quick to disagree, about everything and especially territory.

The disagreements lead to insults.

The insults turned into fist fights.

And before long, one and then another young man would die.

When Mircea was a small boy and he heard the wagons of the other Roma bands, he retreated into the folds of his mother's skirts and begged her to not let them fight.

She shrugged her shoulders. What could she do? Baro Shero was the chief. She had no say.

When Mircea was a little older, he grabbed hold of his father and the other men and begged them not to fight. They shrugged their shoulders. What could they do? It was Baro Shero who demanded they fight. They had no say.

When Mircea was a young man, he approached the leaders of other bands and begged them not to fight. They laughed at him and asked whether he really was a man. The fighting and unnecessary deaths were just a part of life, and nothing they could change.

Mircea's sorrow grew until finally he could stand it no more. He bid farewell to his family and disappeared somewhere deep in the forest. No amount of calling or searching could bring him back. He was gone.

Mircea had always been a gentle soul. But alone in the forest, he grew bitter. Why had they not listened to him? Alone in the forest, he grew angry.

He died. And in his place came a Night Bird with a haunting call.

Some years later, Mircea's band returned to the place where he had disappeared. It felt ominous there, and yet they set up their encampment in the clearing.

That evening, when the chores had been done and the campfire burned, no one sang or danced. They huddled by the fire without saying a word.

It was a young boy who was first to hear the Night Bird call. It seemed to be calling him. He felt he had no choice as he followed the sound of the bird into the forest. By the time his family realized he was gone, it was too late. They couldn't find him.

All wanted to leave that place, and yet there was something that made them stay.

The next night, they huddled around the fire, in silence again. It was a youth who heard the Night Bird call. Now it was calling him. He felt mesmerized as he followed the sound of the bird into the forest. By the time his family realized he was gone, it was too late.

The next day, everyone wanted to leave that bleak place. But Baro Shero, the chief, would not—or could not—budge. He sat all day long with his chin in his hands.

That evening, when the campfire burned, everyone could hear the Night Bird call. Shero jumped up.

"It is for me that the Night Bird calls. It has been after me all along, and it is I who must go. I am sorry for my warring ways; I have done wrong. The Night Bird calls for peace. When I go, so too shall go our warring ways."

Baro Shero walked off into the forest, never to be seen again. After that, as though it were a catchy fiddle tune, peace spread throughout the land. The Russian Roma people began to live in harmony with one another.

Since then, the Night Bird has continued to call, but its call is no longer hypnotic: Its call is a reminder of Shero's pledge for peace.

Let's hope that the Night Bird's call will continue to be heard today and that leaders all around the world hear it. Perhaps we can call with it!

———

EXTENSION   To create the flavor of a Russian Roma circle of caravans, you might frame the story with a traditional song such as "Hai ne ne ne ne" or "Dorogoy Dlinnoyu" ("Those Were the Days, My Friend").

FOR REFLECTION

- What are some important steps for creating peace—at home, in local communities, and around the world?

- What are some situations that prompt a person to take an extreme stance? What examples do you have from your own life?
- When in your life have you known an adult to support a child's vision for change or learn something from a child?

THEMES

activism, anger, anti-oppression, authority, brokenness, calling, change, children, choice, community, conflict, conscience, courage, culture, death, despair, dissent, ethics, evil, failure, governance, grief, guilt, history, honesty, hope, individualism, leadership, listening, mystery, peace, power, pride, purpose, redemption, regret, responsibility, sorrow, suffering, tradition, transcendence, transformation, violence, vision, vulnerability, war

PRINCIPLES

- Acceptance of one another and encouragement to spiritual growth
- Free and responsible search for truth and meaning
- Right of conscience and use of the democratic process
- World community with peace, liberty, and justice for all

STORY MAP

- Roma bands travel around the forest and steppes of Russia.
- Whenever two bands of Roma meet each other, they fight.
- Mircea, a young boy, wants peace between the Roma.
- As a small boy, Mircea begs his mother to make it stop.
- As a youth, he begs his leaders to make it stop.
- As a young adult, he asks other leaders to make it stop.
- Mircea retreats to the forest, alone and bitter.
- He dies in anger and transforms into a Night Bird.
- Years later, the band of Roma returns to the area where Mircea died. They find the camps uncomfortable.
- At nightfall around the campfire, a young boy hears the bird call and follows it.
- No one can find him.
- The next night, an older boy disappears.
- No one can find him. They want to leave, but an older Baro Shero (the chief) refuses.

- Shero contemplates the situation all day.
- Shero hears the bird call and knows it is for him so that the fighting will end.
- Before going, Shero asks his people to pledge to end their fighting ways.
- Peace spreads and continues to this day.

Milk and Sugar

This story is part of the epic poem, Qissa-i Sanjan (The Story of Sanjan) *written in 1599* CE *by Bahman Kaikobad Hamjiar Sanjana. In it, we hear about the challenges of migration and resettlement for an entire population, and we learn that two religious groups can coexist in peace. It is an important story for today, when we live in close proximity to increasing numbers of different cultural groups and continue to need to learn to accept one another.*

WE HUMANS TRAVEL. We move and migrate.

How many of you relocated here from somewhere else? Or perhaps your parents pulled up stakes to come here? Or your grandparents?

We may pack up more often and venture greater distances than previously, but there have always been migrations.

More than three thousand years ago, around 1500 BCE, a prophet was born on the southern steppes of Central Asia. It was somewhere in the region of northwestern Iran or southeastern Afghanistan. His name was Zarathustra, and sometimes he was called Zoroaster.

Zarathustra believed in and preached about one god, and one god only.

He argued that humankind must work for good to prevail over evil. He practiced and preached the virtues of good thought, good word, and good deed.

It took time before his message was accepted. But eventually, many began to follow his teachings. They prayed several times a day, and they worshipped together by lighting fires to both honor and represent god's light and wisdom.

Over time, the Zoroastrians migrated south and east to the valleys of Persia.

There is no record of how they were greeted when they arrived and settled in areas. Perhaps they blended in with the local culture. More likely there was warfare and strife—that was the way of the world back then. Some of the original inhabitants may have fled. Many others converted to the new religion.

Eventually Zoroastrianism flourished and became the dominant religion throughout central Persia for many hundreds of years.

So it was until about 700 CE, when a new group of people arrived in Persia.

They followed another prophet, whose name was Muhammad. Like the Zoroastrians, the Muslims believed in one god and one god only.

Despite their commonalities, the two groups could not understand one another's style of worship. When the Muslims prayed, they turned southwest toward Mecca and bowed down. They did not recognize the Zoroastrians' great fires as a form of prayer, and tried instead to convert them to their own religion.

The Zoroastrians who refused to change had no choice except to flee.

Some of them made their way to the coast. In small boats, they sailed across the Gulfs of Persia and Oman until at last they arrived on the coast of Gujarat, in what is now called India.

Naturally, their landing caused a stir. Word of the new arrivals spread to King Jadav Rana, who came in person to see who they were and what they wanted.

Do you remember what year this was?

700 CE—thirteen hundred years ago!

The Gujaratis and the Zorastrians did not share a spoken language, but they did share a language of symbols. Once the King had understood that the Zoroastrians wanted to stay, he had one of his servants bring a large bowl.

The Zoroastrian priest, the *dastur*, understood that the bowl represented the land of Gujarat.

The king had his servants fill the bowl with milk to the brim, and he bade the dastur taste it.

The dastur understood that this meant the king considered the land of Gujarat to be full already—and sweet as it was. He was undaunted.

He called for his people to bring sugar. As they poured it into the bowl, he stirred. He then invited the king to taste it.

Now the king understood the dastur was arguing that the Zoroastrians wouldn't disturb the well-being of Gujarat. In fact, their presence would make the country sweeter still.

The king retreated to speak with his advisors, and when he returned, he nodded his head. Yes, the Zoroastrians could stay.

Do you remember what year this was?

700 CE—thirteen hundred years ago!

King Jadav Rana's reception of the Zoroastrian refugees was both inclusive and radical. However, he raised three fingers. There were three conditions.

The king recited a small section of a Gujarati poem. He then moved his hand toward the dastur's ears. The priest understood that this meant they must be able to talk together, and that his people must learn the language of Gujarat.

Do you remember what year this was?

700 CE—thirteen hundred years ago!

The dastur appreciated the king's generosity. He was very grateful that they could stay. He nodded his head in agreement—they would learn the language of Gujarat.

I like to imagine that the dastur recited a beautiful poem in Farsi. I like to think it inspired the king and his people to learn the language of the Zoroastrians. What better way to encourage cross-cultural understanding?

If didn't happen then, perhaps it is happening today.

To explain his second condition, the king made the motions of cladding a woman in a sari. The priest understood that this meant the Zoroastrian women must dress in the way of the Gujarati women.

Do you remember what year this was?

700 CE—thirteen hundred years ago!

The priest appreciated the king's openness. He was grateful that they could stay. He nodded his head in agreement.

But I like to think that when the king saw the Parsi women's beautiful robes, he changed his mind and encouraged all styles of dress! What better way to celebrate cross-cultural diversity?

If didn't happen then, perhaps it is happening today.

To explain his third condition, King Jada Rani held his hands together in prayer. One of his servants drew a solid circular line around him.

The dastur understood that this meant his people must respect the religion of the Gujarati people and not try to change it. He also understood that this meant the Hindus would keep their religion to themselves.

The dastur now had one of his people light a flame. He stood beside it, in supplication, as his people drew a solid circular line around him.

The king smiled. He saw that the Zoroastrians would neither proselytize nor interfere. He nodded his head and motioned with his arm. They were welcome to stay in the Kingdom of Gujarat and to continue to worship in their own way.

Do you remember what year this was?

700 CE—thirteen hundred years ago!

I like to imagine that the Hindus and Zoroastrians visited one another's temples and learned about one another's religious practices. What better way to understand and enjoy religious diversity?

If didn't happen then, it is happening today.

The Parsis continue to live in Gujarat, appreciated by and at peace with their Hindu neighbors. They number about 150,000 and make up the largest group who practice Zoroastrianism in the world today.

Imagine, what would have happened to Zoroastrianism if not for King Jadav Rani?

Imagine, what would happen if we all peered deeply into our bowls and recognized the potential sweetness that others can bring?

FOR REFLECTION

- What are some of your experiences of the sweetness of differences?
- What are some ways we can make room for and learn about others?
- What stories do you know about the refugees and their reception? How is this story similar to or different from what is happening today?

THEMES

acceptance, anti-oppression, arrogance, assumptions, authenticity, authority, belief, belonging, community, compassion, conflict, covenant, diversity, empathy, ethics, generosity, God/Goddess, governance, history, hospitality, human rights, identity, inclusion, kindness, leadership, listening, multiculturalism, oppression, peace, privilege, race/ethnicity, religion, respect, rights, vision, war

PRINCIPLES

- Inherent worth and dignity of every person
- Justice, equity, and compassion in human relations
- Acceptance of one another and encouragement to spiritual growth
- Free and responsible search for truth and meaning
- World community with peace, liberty, and justice for all

STORY MAP

- Humans have been migrating forever.
- The prophet Zarathustra was born in south central Asia three thousand years ago.
- He and his followers believed in one god and three important virtues: good thought, good word, and good deed.
- The Zoroastrians pray several times daily and light a fire when worshipping together.
- The religion was slow to be adopted. By about 600 BCE, it flourished in most of present day Iran.
- There is no record of how it spread. It may have been peacefully or by force, as was common then.
- In 700 CE, thirteen hundred years later, Muslims move into Persia.
- Both religions profess there is one god, but the practitioners don't recognize one another's way of worship.
- The Zoroastrians are forced to convert to Islam or flee.
- Some retreat to the coast and sail to Gujarat.
- There, King Janav Radi hears about their arrival and comes to discuss the situation.
- The two leaders use symbolic language to communicate.
- The king has a bowl full of milk, indicating that Gujarat is full and healthy as it is.

230

- The Zoroastrian priest dissolves sugar in milk, indicating that his people won't disturb Gujarat; in fact, they will make it sweeter.
- It is 1,300 years ago, 700 CE. The king suggests the Zoroastrians can stay on three conditions: they learn to speak the local language, they wear local attire, and they do not proselytize.
- The Zoroastrians agree to all conditions. The teller hopes for even more cross-cultural and inter-religious exchange and understanding.
- The two groups have co-existed and thrived for more than thirteen hundred years.

The Blind Man and the Hunter

How does a person become wise? Perhaps by hearing a story like this one, which hails from both West Africa and Zimbabwe. In it, we witness two powerful gifts that make the world a better place: insightful thinking and forgiveness.

FIRST, THERE WAS THE WEDDING, with the kaftans and the headdresses, the drumming and the dancing, the singing and the ululating, the stories and the feasting.

Later, the new husband asked his bride, "Is your brother truly blind?"

"He is."

"But he moves with such grace and confidence."

"He sees with his ears," was her reply.

The husband thought about her words. Perhaps they also explained why it was that, of all the songs sung and poetry recited at the wedding, the blind man's words seemed the wisest.

The husband's claim to fame and source of great pride was his skill at hunting. He went into the bush as often as he could and always came home with supper.

His new brother-in-law often asked if he could join him in the hunt, but the husband was reluctant. Perhaps he was worried that it would be dangerous for a blind man.

One day, the husband came home with a prized gazelle. There was plenty of meat for the entire village. It was delicious!

After the meal, the blind man asked again whether he could join his brother-in-law in the hunt. With a full and satisfied belly, the husband agreed.

The very next morning, the brothers-in-law set off down the trail to set traps for birds. The best place to capture a bird was a long way off.

After they'd been walking for some time the blind man suddenly tugged on the hunter's arm, and whispered, "There's a lion."

"Where?"

"A little ahead and to our left. But it's sleeping, we'll be okay."

Sure enough, they hadn't gone much further when the hunter caught a glimpse of the large buff colored mound, expanding and contracting rhythmically. You know what that was, don't you? Once they'd safely passed it, he asked, "How did you know the lion was there?"

The blind man shrugged, "I see with my ears."

An hour or so later, they arrived at the place where the hunter suggested placing their traps. He set them out. Had anyone been watching, they might have noticed that he took better care to disguise his own trap than that of his brother-in-law's.

The next day, they headed back down the trail to check the traps. After they had walked a ways, the blind man tugged at the hunter's arm once again. "There's an elephant!"

"Where?" demanded the hunter, a little annoyed.

"Up ahead and to our right. It's found a water hole—we need not worry."

Sure enough, after they'd walked a little further, the hunter could make out a wall of wrinkled gray. You know what that was, don't you?

Once they'd safely passed it, he asked, "How did you know the elephant was there?"

Again, the blind man shrugged, "I see with my ears."

They walked on, and even before they had arrived at the traps, the blind man shouted with exuberance, "We've caught some birds!"

The hunter went to his own trap first. He had caught a small gray bird. He released it from the trap and put it in his pouch.

As he approached the blind man's trap, his heart beat faster and his head began to spin with jealousy. The blind man's trap held a dazzling bird whose long tail feathers were a rainbow of colors! Quickly, the hunter grabbed the bird and, with a slight-of-hand, he gave the blind man the gray bird and put the rainbow bird in his own pouch.

As they walked home, the hunter began to think about his wife's face and how it would light up when he gave her the beautiful bird he had captured.

Thinking about his wife caused him to recall their wedding—the dances, the songs, the poetry. And he thought again about the wisdom of his brother-in-law.

Suddenly it occurred to him that here on the trail was his opportunity to learn more from this sage. So he said to his brother-in-law, "You are so clever, tell me why, when there is so much beauty in this world, that there is also hatred and war?"

It was a few moments before the blind man answered, "Strife and war are caused by the kind of dishonesty and greed that you have just displayed."

The hunter gulped. He searched for words to explain his actions, but even the excuse of taking the bird for his wife's sake felt shallow. Instead, he took the rainbow bird out of his pouch and exchanged it for the blind man's gray bird.

They walked along some more and the hunter resumed his questioning. "How is it that war can ever end?"

Now the blind man smiled. He said, "Strife disappears and peace returns when people learn from their mistakes and change their ways, just as you have just done."

The hunter breathed a sigh of relief. They walked home in silence.

After that, whenever anyone asked why the blind man was so wise his brother-in-law, the hunter, would say, "Because he sees with his ears, and hears with his heart."

FOR REFLECTION

- Can you recall a time when you mistakenly made assumptions about another person's abilities?
- What examples do you know of greed preventing a person from perceiving the truth?
- How has the experience of being forgiven for an error in judgment affected your life?

THEMES

arrogance, assumptions, belonging, character, choice, conflict, conscience, discernment, ethics, family, forgiveness, generosity, greed, growth, guilt, honesty, humility, identity, integrity, justice, leadership, limitations, reconciliation, redemption, respect, self-respect, shame, trust, vulnerability

PRINCIPLES

- Inherent worth and dignity of every person
- Justice, equity, and compassion in human relations
- Free and responsible search for truth and meaning
- World community with peace, liberty, and justice for all

STORY MAP

- There is a wedding.
- Later, the husband asks if the wife's wise brother truly is blind.
- She replies, "He sees with his ears."

- The husband is very proud of his hunting skills. The blind brother-in-law wants to go hunting, but the husband refuses to take him.
- Feeling proud after he has fed the entire village with the bounty from his own hunting, the husband invites his wife's brother to go hunting.
- The next day, the two men head out to set traps for birds.
- The hunter's brother-in-law is the first to be aware of a lion. He explains that he sees with his ears.
- The hunter sets the traps. The two walk home.
- Next day, they return to check the traps.
- The brother-in-law is the first to be aware of an elephant. He explains that he sees with his ears.
- Before they arrive in the clearing, the brother-in-law knows they've been successful.
- The hunter rushes to retrieve the birds. He finds a gray bird in his trap and puts it in his pouch.
- He finds a colorful bird in the trap he set for his brother-in-law but wants it!
- He moves the gray bird from his pouch to his brother-in-law's pouch and keeps the colorful one.
- As they walk back, the hunter recalls the brother-in-law's wisdom and asks, "Why is there war?"
- The brother-in-law replies, "Because people do as you have just done."
- The hunter is embarrassed. He quietly switches the birds back.
- Later, the hunter asks, "How can there ever be peace?"
- The brother-in-law replies, "Peace is restored when people do as you have just done."
- Later, the hunter describes his brother-in-law as wise because he sees with his ears and hears with his heart.

Pandora's Gift

Retelling this classic Greek myth in a way that emphasizes hope over evil is an excellent antidote to the culture of fear that dominates much of North America. As the Chinese Proverb goes, "It is better to light a candle than to curse the darkness." Pandora's story might be told to honor someone who has brought hope by working to make the world a better place, or inspired cheer on a dark night.

LONG AGO, when the world was so brand new that there was still a bit of sheen on it, the gods looked down at Earth. Suddenly they realized they'd made a terrible mistake.

The gods themselves were a widely diverse group. Some were tall and thin; others were short and wide; some had hair that was blond and curly; others had hair that was dark and straight. More dramatically, some were male, others were female, and a few were a bit of both.

Yet, when the gods had fashioned humans, they'd made only a single gender, only man. How boring was that? What about their own sister Aphrodite? They had forgotten to make a single human modeled on her feminine qualities. How could they have made a mistake like that?

So the gods got to work, carefully modeling and shaping the clay to look just like Aphrodite. They fussed and they worried.

They wanted their new creation to be beautiful and good. They wanted her to be lovely and kind.

When they were finally finished making this first woman, she was gorgeous. When they breathed life into her, she was filled with goodness and passion. They called her Pandora and gave her a special and challenging job.

The gods wanted Pandora to keep guard over everything that was her opposite. They wanted her to keep all that was *not* beautiful and good, lovely and kind from tainting the world.

They took hatred, anger, greed, jealousy, despair, sorrow, suffering, pain, illness—all that was evil—and plunged it into a big, beautifully decorated urn. They closed the urn with a tightly fitted cork and sealed it with wax.

They gave the urn to Pandora and commanded her *not* to open it. They sent her off to live in the lower realms, where we humans dwell, and rubbed their hands together in satisfaction. All was well and as it should be—Pandora would keep the lid on all the evils of the world. The gods could relax.

Pandora placed the lovely urn in a corner of her room. For a while, she was so busy getting used to being alive that she forgot all about it.

But now and then, when her eyes happened to drift to that corner of her room, she would wonder what was inside that urn, and what would happen were she to open it.

If you'd been given a gift and told not to open it, wouldn't you be curious?

Opening it just a crack, surely that wouldn't hurt.

Should she do it? What do you think? Yes? No?

One day, she suddenly thought, "Why not?" She opened it. Immediately, it was too late! The deed was done. Out flew darkness and fear, jealousy and anger, greed and hatred. All the evils flew out into the world.

She tried to catch them and push them back into the urn. They moved with such force that Pandora could barely press the lid back down. But it was impossible. It was hopeless.

Or so it seemed at first. But as she sat there, wondering what to do, she heard something tinkling inside the urn. Something had not escaped. The sound was gentle. What was it?

Pandora opened the urn just a crack more and what she saw put a smile on her face.

What she saw was a glimmer of hope. She opened the lid a little wider. Hope flew up and out into the world and spread its bright light everywhere.

Surely, if hope can survive in an urn filled with all the evils in the world, then there is reason for us all to feel hopeful.

FOR REFLECTION

- What do you do to restore hope when all seems lost?
- When has a glimmer of hope been transformational for you?
- What impacts have you noticed when you have changed a story? This could be a traditional tale you prefer to retell in a new way, or it could be a story from your own life that can be told more than one way.

THEMES

anger, choice, despair, evil, failure, fear, God/Goddess, greed, grief, guilt, hope, peace, shame, sorrow, suffering, vision, worry

PRINCIPLES

- Inherent worth and dignity of every person
- Justice, equity, and compassion in human relations
- Acceptance of one another and encouragement to spiritual growth
- World community with peace, liberty, and justice for all

- The world is still very new when the gods realize they've made a mistake.
- Although they gave the world many different forms of life, they have forgotten to make a human in the image of their beautiful sister.
- They use clay. The work is fussy. They want her to be beautiful, lovely, good, and kind.
- When they are satisfied, they call her Pandora and give her a job.
- They put all that is Pandora's opposite into an urn and seal it tightly.
- They deliver Pandora and the urn to earth, warning her not to open it.
- At first, she is too busy to care. Eventually, she grows curious.
- She opens the urn just a crack. When she sees evil spilling out, she tries to close the urn but can't until after the evil has escaped.
- Pandora worries.
- She hears something else rattling inside the urn.
- She open it a crack and sees a glimmer of hope. She releases it.
- Hope spreads throughout the world.
- If hope can survive in an urn full of evil, surely it can also thrive in us.

Sources

Children of Darkness

Reed, A.W. *Myths and Legends of Maoriland*. Wellington, NZ: A.H. and A.W. Reed, 1947.

The Encyclopedia of New Zealand. "Story: Te Waonui a Tāne—Forest Mythology" by Te Ahukaramū Charles Royal. teara.govt.nz/en/te-waonui -a-tane-forest-mythology

The Voice of the Great Spirit

Fahs, Sophia Lyon and Alice Cobb. *Old Tales for a New Day*. Buffalo, NY: Prometheus Press, 1980.

Unaipon, David, Stephen Muecke, ed., and Adam Shoemaker, ed. *Legendary Tales of the Australian Aborigines*. Melbourne: Melbourne University Press, 2001.

The Priest in Paradise

Philip, Neil and Jacqueline Mair. *Horse Hooves and Chicken Feet: Mexican Folktales*. New York: Clarion Books, 2003.

The Noble Deer

Iyengar, Smt. Vatsala and S.W. Khatai. *Panchantantra*. Bangalore: Vasau Publications, 2008.

The Great Hunter from Aluk

Bak, Ove. *Troldbjørnen: også isbjørne har en sjæl: beretninger og fortællinger fra Grønland*. København, DK: Hernov, 1979.

Kaalund, Bodil. *The Art of Greenland: Sculpture, Crafts, Painting*, translated by Kenneth Tindall. Berkeley, CA: University of California Press, 1983.

Rasmussen, Knud. *Myter og Sagn fra Grønland: Vestgrønland,* Vol. 2. Copenhagen: Gyldendal, 1924.

Baldy

Kvideland, Reimund and Henning K. Sehmsdorf, eds. *Scandinavian Folk Belief and Legend*. Minneapolis: University of Minnesota Press, 1988.

To Whom Does the Land Belong?

Jaffre, Nina and S. Zeitlin. *Riddle Stories and Justice Tales from Around the World*. New York: Henry Holt, 1998.

Yashinsky, Dan. *Tales for an Unknown City: Tales from One Thousand and One Friday Nights of Storytelling*. Toronto: McGill-Queen's University Press, 1990.

The Hole Boy

Evans, I. H. N. *The Religion of the Tempasuk Dusuns of North Borneo*. New York: Cambridge University Press, 2012.

Fahs, Sophia Lyon and Alice Cobb. *Old Tales for a New Day*. Buffalo, NY: Prometheus, 1980.

Mahdi, Louise Carus, Nancy Geyer Christopher, and Michael Mead, eds. *Crossroads: The Quest for Contemporary Rites of Passage*. Peru, IL: Open Court Publishing, 1996.

Punzak, Michael, E. Brody, Jay Goldspinner et al., eds. *Spinning Tales, Weaving Hope: Stories Of Peace, Justice & the Environment*. Philadelphia: New Society, 1992.

Vasilisa, the Brave

Evetts-Secker, Josephine. *Mother and Daughter Tales*. Richmond Hill, VA: Abbeville Kids, 1996.

SurLaLune. "The Annotated Baba Yaga." surlalunefairytales.com/babayaga/index.html

Crow and Partridge

Barrows Dutton, Maude. *The Tortoise and the Geese and Other Fables of Bidpai*. Boston and New York: Houghton Mifflin Co., 1908. mainlesson.com/display.php?author=Dutton&book=tortoise&story=partridge

The Happy Man's Shirt

Calvino, Italo. *Italian Folktales*. New York: Pantheon, 1980.

Granny's Ride

Briggs, Katharine M. and Ruth L. Tongue, eds. *Folktales of England*. Chicago: University of Chicago Press, 1967.

Keding, Dan. *Elder Tales: Stories of Wisdom and Courage from Around the World*. Westport, CT: Libraries Unlimited, 2008.

Trustworthy Traveler

Aulia's World. "Hazrat Sheikh Abdul Qadir Jilani," auliasworld.com/2011/07/hazrat-sheikh-abdul-qadir-jilani-ra.html

Conover, Sarah and Freda Crane. *Ayat Jamilah Beautiful Signs: A Treasury of Islamic Wisdom for Children and Parents*. Boston: Skinner House Books, 2011.

Ivarr's Tale

Magnusson, Magnus, trans. and ed. *The Icelandic Sagas*. London: The Folio Society, 1999.

Bolsover and Associates. "The King Who Listened" by Alexander Linklater. bolsover-psychology.co.uk/psychotherapy.htm

The Online Medieval and Classical Library. "Heimskringla or the Chronicle of the Kings of Norway: Saga of Sigurd the Crusader and His Brothers Eystein and Olaf." http://omacl.org/Heimskringla/crusaders.html

The Meat of the Tongue

Baltuck, Naomi. *Apples from Heaven: Multicultural Folk Tales About Stories and Storytellers*. North Haven, CT: Linnet Books, 1995.

Forest, Heather. *Wisdom Tales from Around the World*. Little Rock, AR: August House, 2005.

Knappert, Jan. *Myths and Legends of the Swahili*. London: Heinemann Educational Books, 1970.

The Elephant and the Dog

Cultural India. "The Elephant and the Dog." culturalindia.net/indian-folktales/jataka-tales/elephant-and-dog.html

Williams, Marcia. *The Elephant's Friend and Other Tales from Ancient India*. Somerville, MA: Candlewick Press, 2012.

Birds Learn about Friendship

Htin Aung, Maung. *Burmese Folk Tales*. New Delhi: Oxford University Press, 1948.

Macdonald, Margaret Read. *Peace Tales: World Folktales to Talk About*. Hamden, CT: Linnet Books, 1992.

Polite Peculiarities

Ragan, Kathleen. *Fearless Girls, Wise Women and Beloved Sisters*. New York: Norton, 2000.

Fielde, Adele M. *Chinese Nights' Entertainment*. New York: G.P. Putnam's Sons, 1893.

The Sign of the Tassel

Jamali, Sarah Powell. *Folktales from the City of the Golden Domes*. Beirut: Khayats Booksellers and Publishers, 1965.

Ragan, Kathleen. *Fearless Girls, Wise Women and Beloved Sisters: Heroines in Folktales from Around the World*. New York: Norton, 2000.

Kassa, the Strong One

Courlander, Harold. *The Cow Tail Switch and Other West African Stories*. New York: Henry Holt, 1974.

The Magic Spring

Keding, Dan. *Elder Tales: Stories of Wisdom and Courage from Around the World*. Westport, CT: Libraries Unlimited, 2008.

Rhee, Nami. *Magic Spring*. New York: Putnam, 1993.

A Gift for Grandfather

Courlander, Harold. *The King's Drum and Other African Stories*. New York: Harcourt, Brace & World, 1962.

Gordh, Bill. *Stories in Action*. Westport, CT: Libraries Unlimited, 2006.

MacDonald, Margaret Read. *Earth Care*. Northaven, CT: Linnet Books, 1999.

Ukko's Bread

Livo, Norma J. and George Livo. *The Enchanted Wood and Other Tales from Finland*. Englewood, CO: Evergreen Publishing Group, 1999.

Uexpress. "Tell Me a Story: Ukko's Bread (A Folktale from Finland)." uexpress.com/tell-me-a-story/2008/5/25/ukkos-bread-a-folktale-from-finland

Primroses for Gold

Briggs, Katharine M. and Ruth L. Tongue. *Folktales of England.* Chicago: University of Chicago Press, 1965.

Generosity Bends the Road

Lufti Abdallah, Ali. *The Clever Sheikh of the Butana and Other Stories: Sudanese Folk Tales* (International Folk Tales Series). Northampton, MA: Interlink Books, 1999.

Cultural Information about Sudan. sudan.net

The Drum

Ramanujan, A.K. *Folktales from India: A Selection of Oral Tales from Twenty-two Languages.* New York: Pantheon Books, 1991.

The South Asian. thesouthasian.org/archives/2003/a_drum_an_indian_folk _tale.html

The Gentleman and the Thief

Fielde, Adele M. *Chinese Nights' Entertainment.* New York: G.P. Putnam's Sons, 1893.

Jenkins, Roger. "The Thief and the Mask." rogerjenkins.com.sg/thiefandmask .html

The Jug on the Rock

DeSpain, Pleasant. *Thirty-three Multicultural Tales to Tell.* Little Rock, AR: August House, 1993.

Shelton, A.L. *Tibetan Folktales.* St. Louis, MO: United Christian Missionary Society, 1925.

Sacred Texts. "The Story of the Donkey and the Rock (A Black Tent Story)." sacred-texts.com/asia/tft/tft07.htm

Strength in Unity

Babbitt, Ellen C. *Jataka Tales.* New York: The Century Company, 1912.

Iyengar, S.V. and S.W. Khatai. *Panchatantra.* Bangalore, India: Vasan Publications, 2008.

Cultural India. "The Hunter and the Doves." www.culturalindia.net/indian -folktales/Panchatantra-tales/unity-is-strength.html

McLoughlin, Margo. *Seeds of Generosity, Storytelling in the Classroom.* Victoria, BC: Salisbury House Press, 2012.

Sister Goose and the Foxes

Ragan, Kathleen, ed. *Outfoxing Fear.* New York: W. W. Norton, 2006.

Tidwell, John Edgar and Steven C. Tracy, eds. *After Winter: The Art and Life of Sterling A. Brown.* New York: Oxford University Press, 2009.

Brother Fox and the Geese

About.com: Classic Literature. "The Fox and the Geese by The Brothers Grimm," translated by Margaret Taylor. http://classiclit.about.com/library/bl-etexts/grimm/bl-grimm-foxgeese.htm

Grimm, Jacob and Wilhelm. *The Original Folk and Fairy Tales of the Brothers Grimm.* Princeton, NJ: Princeton University Press, 2015.

Two Pebbles

de Bono, Edward. *Lateral Thinking: Creativity Step by Step.* New York: Harper Perennial, 1970.

The Bell of Justice

Longfellow, Henry Wadsworth. *Tales of a Wayside Inn: Part Second.* Boston: Houghton Mifflin Company, 1915.

"The Bell of Justice: Folktales of Aarne-Thompson-Uther type 207C," selected and edited by D.L. Ashliman. pitt.edu/~dash/type0207c.html#gestaromanorum

The Fifty-Dollar Bill

Briggs, Katharine M. and Ruth L. Tongue. *Folktales of England.* Chicago: University of Chicago Press, 1965.

Brunvand, Jan Harold. *Encyclopedia of Urban Legends, Updated and Expanded Edition: A–L.* Santa Barbara, California: ABC-CLIO, LLC, 2012.

Gillett, Frederick. "The Fifty Dollar Bill." Indianapolis: *Sunday Star*, March 3, 1946.

The Magnificent Red Bud Tree

The Baldwin Project: Bringing Yesterday's Classics to Today's Children. "More Jataka Tales" by Ellen C. Babbitt. mainlesson.com

Francis, H.T. and E.J. Thomas, eds. "The Judas Tree" in *Jataka Tales, Selected and Edited with Introduction and Notes.* Cambridge University Press, 1916.

Crow and Pitcher

Tales with Morals. taleswithmorals.com/aesop-fable-the-crow-and-the-pitcher .htm

Aesop and Robert Temple. *The Complete Fables*. London: Penguin Classics, 1998.

One Thousand Ideas, One Idea

Carey, Bonnie. *Baba Yaga's Geese and Other Russian Stories*. Bloomington: Indiana University Press, 1973.

The Monkey Who Asked for Misery

Wolkenstein, Diane. *The Magic Orange Tree and Other Haitian Folktales*. New York: Schocken, 1978.

The Shining Jewel

Crottet, Robert. *The Enchanted Forest*. London: The Richards Press, Ltd., 1949.

Grandfather and Grandson

Grimm, Jacob and Wilhelm. *The Original Folk and Fairy Tales of the Brothers Grimm*. Princeton, NJ: Princeton University Press, 2015.

Yolen, Jane. *Favorite Folktales from Around the World*. New York: Pantheon Books, 1986.

Donald of the Burdens

Warner, Gerald. *Tales of the Scottish Highlands*. London: Shepheard-Walwyn, 1982.

Beirhorst, John, ed. *Latin American Folktales: Stories from Hispanic and Indian Traditions*. New York: Pantheon Fairy Tale and Folklore Library, 2002.

Capturing Spring

Nottingham Hidden History Team. "The Wise Men of Gotham" by Frank E. Earp. https://nottinghamhiddenhistoryteam.wordpress.com/2014/ 01/16/the-wise-men-of-gotham

Internet Sacred Text Archive. "The Wise Men of Gotham." sacred-texts.com/ neu/eng/meft/meft44.htm

A Pig's Life

Radice, William, ed. *Myths and Legends of India*. London: Folio, 2001.

Ramanujan, A.K. *Folktales from India: A Selection of Oral Tales from Twenty-two Languages*. New York: Pantheon Books, 1991.

The Almond Tree

Spirit of Trees. "Honi and the Carob Tree: A Talmud Tale" retold by Peninnah
Schram. http://spiritoftrees.org/honi-and-the-carob-tree

MacDonald, Margaret Read. *Earth Care: World Folktales to Talk About.* North
Haven, CT: 1999.

Cooking Together, Trinidad Style

Boomert, Arie. *The Indigenous Peoples of Trinidad and Tobago from the First
Settlers Until Today.* Leiden, The Netherlands: Sidestone Press, 2016.
sidestone.com/library/the-indigeous-peoples-of-trinidad-and-tobago

Joseph, Lynn. *The Mermaid's Twin Sister.* New York: Clarion Books, 1994.

Hannah and the Wind

"The Clothesline" in *Jewish Tales of Holy Women* by Yitzhak Buxbaum. http://
learningtogive.org/resources/folktales/Clotheslines.asp

The Night Bird

Riordan, James, ed. *Russian Gypsy Tales; Collected by Yefim Druts and Alexei
Gessler.* New York: Interlink Press, 1992.

Milk and Sugar

Delhi Parsis. "The Story of Sanjan: Kissa-i-Sanjan." http://delhiparsis.com/
2007/08/19/the-story-of-sanjan-kissa-i-sanjan

The History of Zoroastrianism. www.bbc.co.uk/religion/religions/zoroastrian/
ataglance/glance.shtml

"Milk and Sugar—a legend told by Jill Lamede, the Tintagel Storyteller." you-
tube.com/watch?v=3hrEsdGXzco

The Blind Man and the Hunter

Lupton, Hugh. *Tales of Wisdom and Wonder.* Cambridge, MA: Barefoot Books,
1998.

McCall Smith, Alexander. *The Girl Who Married a Lion and Other Tales From
Africa.* New York: Pantheon Books, 2004.

McLoughilin, Margo. *Seeds of Generosity, Storytelling in the Classroom.* Victoria, BC: Salisbury House Press, 2012.

Pandora's Gift

Strauss, Kevin. *Tales with Tails: Storytelling the Wonders of the Natural World.*
Westport, CT: Libraries Unlimited, 2006.

Thematic Index

Anger

Animals

Anti-oppression

Arrogance

Assumptions

Brokenness

Calling

Caring

Change

Character

Children

Choice

Class

Coming of Age

Commitment

254

Conscience

Contemplation

Courage

Covenant

Creativity

Culture

Inclusion

Individualism

Integrity

Interdependence

Intuition

Journey

Joy

Justice

Kindness

Leadership

Letting Go

Limitations

Listening

Love

Loyalty

Marriage

Mentorship

Redemption

Regret

Relationships

Religion

Respect

Responsibility

Revelation

Reverence

Rights

Ritual

Sacred

Sacrifice

Searching

Self-acceptance

Self-care

Teamwork

Tradition

Transcendence

Transformation

Trust

Truth

Unity

Violence

Vision

Vulnerability

War

Weakness

Youth

Principle Index

The inherent worth and dignity of every person

Justice, equity, and compassion in human relations

Acceptance of one another and encouragement to spiritual growth

A free and responsible search for truth and meaning

Right of conscience and use of the democratic process

World community with peace, liberty, and justice for all

Respect for the interdependent web of all existence

Acknowledgments

There is a trust exercise where several people spread their arms out vertically and together hold another person in the air. It's a wonderful sensation! I feel as though I am that person, carried along by an immense circle of support. It was the encouragement of many people and the path many of them have walked before me that enabled me to write this book.

There are the ancient griots, bards, and shanachies. There are story collectors that span the ages: from Vishnu Sharma to Homer to Snorri Sturluson, from the Grimm brothers to Calvino to Grundtvig, and from Knud Rasmussen to Katherine Briggs to Kathleen Ragan. There are storytelling revivalists like Diane Wolkenstein, Margaret Read MacDonald, Doug Lipman, and Alice Kane who, together with many others, paved the wonderful oral storytelling path that I've followed. Melanie Ray and Nan Gregory deserve special mention as my first-ever storytelling workshop leaders who continue to inspire me with their skills.

Though she passed away before it was complete, throughout the writing of this book my heart reverberated with the faith my mother had in me, and I'm certain that my father Hugh's yarn-spinning style shines through in some of the tales. I am deeply grateful for the keen and honest feedback from my husband, Christian Engelstoft, and our three children—Kaya, Nadia and Emil—who patiently listened to many of the stories and offered their reflections. A big salute to my storytelling sister Karen Gummo and our conversations, which have long enriched my approach to story. Heartfelt thanks to my long-time "story buddy," Margo McLoughlin, whose expansive knowledge of folktales and gentle perceptiveness always helps me improve my work. I appreciate her making me aware of "The Drum" and "Jug on the Rock," welcome additions to this collection.

Mary Benard, my enthusiastic and discerning editor, was a joy to work with. I am grateful for the support and wisdom offered by the Reverends Melora and Shana Lynngood, ministers at the First Unitarian Church of Victoria. Members of the Unitarian Church of Victoria, the Victoria Storyteller's Guild, and my liberal religious education colleagues from across Canada have inspired me, and I am indebted to many of them for responding reflectively to my stories. I appreciate "Storytell" listserve members Jill Lamede and Richard Martin for making me aware of the Parsi story "Milk and Sugar" when they initiated a discussion about it, and Daire Seaman and several others for their perceptive comments. In October of 2014, I was fortunate to attend a storytelling session when Wedlidli Speck, hereditary chief of the G'ixsam Clan of the Kwakiutl Nation proper, happened to tell "Half Boy." It was a pleasure to hear another variation of this thought-provoking tale and have a chance to hear his insights. Penny Draper offered the innovative solution of calling my version "Hole Boy." Colleagues, friends, and family—too many to name—energized me with their interest in the book, and I thank them all! In particular, I offer my gratitude to Janet Gray, who strongly reinforced my inclination to include material that explores our sense of place and our relationship with the natural world.

The First Unitarian Church of Victoria was most generous in granting me a short sabbatical so that I could finish the book without distraction. I am especially indebted to Anna Isaacs and LeAnn Andersen for covering for me during my absence from work, and there were many others who helped as well. Karen George was a lifesaver when she lent me her computer when mine suddenly expired. Adriana Ramirez and Wayne Adams, my hosts at Condominium Carrazillilo, were exceptionally kind and the sisters and staff at Bethlehem Retreat Centre were very caring. In these two special places, I found the peace and quiet needed to focus on writing.

The good will of those I've named and countless others has been truly heartwarming. Their acts of generosity confirm for me that the stories are true in the deepest sense and that the spirit of compassion remains alive and well today.